The Restored King

The Fallen King Chronicles Book 4

RICHARD FIERCE

ebook ISBN: 978-1-947329-01-0
Print ISBN-13: 978-1-947329-00-3

CONTENTS

ACKNOWLEDGMENTS

A huge thank you to my wife.
Her endless support is priceless.

—Jovanna

CHAPTER 1

Garrick opened his eyes.

His head was pounding with a powerful headache and the front of his face felt swollen. He blinked a few times and stared at the unfamiliar ceiling above him. *Where am I?* he wondered.

Hearing movement to the left, he turned his head to see an old man in robes. The man was standing beside a closed door that looked like it was made of gold, his arms crossed over his chest. His robes were white and trimmed in silver. Garrick squinted and thought the man was looking at him, but he wasn't sure.

With great effort, he pushed himself up to a sitting position and looked around the room. It was fairly large and had beds that were spaced evenly throughout. Garrick counted six in total, including his. The other beds were empty, their sheets pulled tightly in place and tucked under the edges. The walls appeared to be white marble striated with blue and black lines. Alternating triangular tiles of teal and blue created an interesting pattern on the floor.

Garrick reached up and began rubbing his temples with his index fingers, hoping it might help relieve his headache. It didn't. The old man at the door hadn't moved the entire time, though Garrick suspected the man was watching him like a hawk.

"Where am I?" Garrick finally asked. His voice sounded odd and nasally. Was his nose broken?

"The Temple of Zevea." The old man's response was so quiet, Garrick almost didn't hear him.

"How … how did I get here?" he asked. Fear clenched his stomach. He tried to remember what might have happened, but it was a dark blur in the back of his mind. The old man didn't answer. A few moments later, the door swung open and a familiar face greeted him. It was Kelvin. He was dressed like the old man in the same flowing robes.

"Come with me," he said.

"Why am I here?" Garrick asked.

"I'll explain on the way. Follow me."

Garrick stood up on shaky legs. He hesitated, fearing his legs might give out on him. When they didn't, he took a few steps. Satisfied, he walked out of the room and followed Kelvin. The man's robes billowed around him as he walked at a brisk pace. Garrick kept up as best as he could. The hall they walked through was identical to the room he had just left. Every door they passed was gold and glinted in the strange light that came from spheres hanging at various intervals.

"How did we get here?" Garrick asked as they walked.

"You don't remember?"

"No."

"Well … it's probably best that you don't. I knocked you out."

Garrick's face scrunched in confusion. "Why?"

Kelvin cleared his throat. "I apologized before I did

it, if that means anything to you. I didn't mean to hit you as hard as I did, but I managed to break your nose." They continued walking in silence before Kelvin spoke again. "There was an army of elves coming toward us. We had nowhere to go and you were ready to die fighting. I'm blessed by Zevea with a unique talent. I can … travel … far distances in mere moments."

"What does that have to do with hitting me?"

"The power only works with one conscious person. It's a blessing for those called to hunt down agents of Mordum. We can travel with someone, but they can't be conscious."

"Why not?" Garrick asked.

"It would kill them. We are not invincible with our armor, and I did not feel like dying. So, I took the only other option I could think of. And I brought us here."

"Where is here, exactly?"

"The location of this temple is a closely guarded secret. I'm afraid I cannot tell you … my Lord."

"I see."

They stopped at the end of the hall in front of two tall golden doors. Garrick wondered if they were really made of gold. Kelvin easily pushed them open.

"Not real gold," Garrick muttered to himself.

"It's real gold," Kelvin replied. "The gold is only a coating over the wood beneath. If they were full gold, I doubt I'd be able to budge them. Even with my armor."

Garrick nodded in silent agreement and they stepped into the doorway. The room they entered was no differently designed than the hall or the previous room. Several robed priests stood guard along the walls that led toward a raised floor. In the center of the rise sat an unadorned throne. As they approached, Garrick could tell the chair was old. The wood was smooth from wear. It had a tall back and two armrests. It was lacquered and seemed to shine when the light hit it just right.

Sitting on the throne was a woman. As soon as Garrick noticed, his entire focus rested on her. She was one of the most beautiful women he had ever seen, and he had seen many. Her hair was brown and spilled down over her shoulders, the ends reaching her waist. She sat straight with perfect posture, reminding Garrick of many of the nobles in his court.

Kelvin stopped right before the raised floor and bowed low. Not wanting to be rude, Garrick did the same. The faint smell of lavender reached his nose. His eyes met hers for long moments. Neither said anything. Garrick felt as though he could stare into her eyes forever and never grow weary of their green depths.

"King Garrick," she finally greeted. "It is good to finally meet you face to face."

"My Lady," Garrick replied. "I would honor your name, but I do not know it."

"You may call me Laracova," she paused, "Prophet of Zevea."

Garrick's fear returned. Why would the rival Prophet of Mordum summon him? He glanced uneasily between Laracova and Kelvin. Nothing about their attitude or posture seemed hostile. Still, he had a bad feeling.

"How can I be of assistance to you?" he asked.

"Please, calm your emotions," Laracova said. "I can sense your chaotic feelings and they are disturbing my calm. You have nothing to fear from me or anyone else here."

Her tone did calm him somewhat. "My apologies," he said. "I'm sure it is obvious whose mark I bear, though I do not follow his ways. I am curious to know why I am here."

Laracova smiled at him disarmingly. "Kelvin did what he thought was the best course of action, given the situation. While I may disagree with him, the point is moot since you are already here within our walls. I did not ask him to bring you here," she said. Leaning forward, she motioned him closer.

He took a few steps closer, but did not step onto the stairs that led up the platform.

"I want to be of service to you," she said. "I know the peril your kingdom faces. The elves are a formidable enemy. I offer you the strength of our warrior priests."

Garrick considered her words. "Why?" he finally asked.

"I have heard tale of your honor," she answered, glancing briefly to Kelvin. "You care for your people as a good king should. I had my doubts about your intentions, especially when I learned you were one of Mordum's servants." She held up a hand to still his argument. "Yet Zevea has commanded me to assist you regarding this matter. While we may only see the outside of men, the gods see the inside."

That truth resonated within him. "Indeed they do," he said.

"Once the elves have been dealt with, my priests are to report to Oakhaven."

"The capital of Oakvalor?" Garrick asked. "What's in Oakhaven?"

Laracova stood from her throne and descended the steps. "Come, walk with me in the garden."

She led the way out of the chamber, and Garrick fell into step beside her. Kelvin followed behind them, though he kept a respectful distance.

"What do you know of Mordum's intent? Does that mark give you insight into his mind?"

"No," Garrick said. "I have not received anything other than the armor and the blade."

"A pity," she said. "While the gods know the thoughts of men, they do not know the thoughts of gods. Zevea has told me that something is coming. Darkness. War." The hall they walked through split to either side and she turned them to the right. A door, plain and unadorned, led them outside. Walking down a few flagstone steps, they entered the garden.

It was a large area built in terraces along the sloping face of a mountain. Garrick tried to guess their location by the landscape, but quickly gave up. The scenery was as foreign as the elves at his gates. Ornamental shrubs and ponds surrounded small tinkling fountains. Orchids and roses and trailing vines covered stone archways. Paths led between carefully carved hedges and into shady grottos. The garden, exceedingly beautiful, served several functional purposes as well. In the center of the top level, where they were standing, was a large ornamental pond. The aura of tranquility struck Garrick immediately. It was quiet except for the occasional chirping of a few multi-colored birds.

"This place is breathtaking," Garrick said softly, fearing that his words might somehow impact the peace of the garden.

"Thank you," Laracova said. "Its beauty is deceptive. This garden is a fortification. Tunnels run the length of each terrace, with grated openings in strategic locations. It allows us the advantage of being in all places at once."

Garrick nodded, admiring the beauty of the garden as well as the hidden function of it. *She must trust me,* he thought. *Why else would she share that secret?*

She led them to the pond in the center. A few large coy fish swam lazily. A short pillar held a silver bowl atop it. Reaching into the bowl, Laracova grabbed a handful of bread crumbs and tossed them into pond. The fish fought each other for the pieces, disrupting the calm surface of the water.

"The pond reminds me of the world," she said. "The surface is calm from the outside, but underneath there is turbulence. And every so often, that turbulence affects the surface. I think it is evident to all of us in faith, but the gods are at war. Mankind is about to be brought into the conflict, with or without our consent. Mordum seeks a mortal body to wage his war here among us."

"I've heard the rumors," Garrick acknowledged. "How much truth there is to them, I don't know."

"In every rumor, there is a seed of truth. Yet they are more than rumors, Lord Garrick. Even now, Mordum's servants seek out the remains of his previous body. War is on the horizon. Where do you stand, I wonder?"

Garrick wondered that himself. He would do whatever he had to in order to protect his people. If Mordum's plans included keeping Talvaard safe, then his lot was with the dark god. And if Mordum's warpath were to consume his kingdom … Garrick paused the thought in his mind. Would he—*could* he—stand against Mordum? He bore the god's mark, after all. And he has seen the Prophet take control of men with the mark, watched as men with no inhibitions killed and destroyed their own loved ones. He rubbed at the thin material that hid the mark.

"I will do what is right," he finally answered.

Laracova stared at him with a piercing gaze. "I'm sure that you will. I have heard that you allied yourself with the prince of Oakvalor."

"I have," Garrick said. "His support was pivotal for my claim to the throne. As such, I am in debt to him."

"Then you shall march to Oakhaven as well?"

Garrick looked at her, confused.

"One of Mordum's servants currently sits on the throne in Oakhaven. From what my priests tell me, he has made it an all-important mission to bring Mordum into our plane of existence. He must be stopped. I hear that the prince you call your ally is on the path, ready to stand in the way of Mordum's goals. He walks a dangerous road and there are few strong enough to offer him aide. So, I ask again. You shall march to

Oakhaven?"

"I will do what I can to help," Garrick answered evasively. "Right now, my sole concern is for the safety of my people. Once we drive the elves back, I can focus on helping others."

"I understand," Laracova said. "As I said, you have the support of my warriors. They are ready to travel when you are."

"Thank you." Garrick watched the fish cease their fighting. They resumed swimming, moving about the pond slowly.

Laracova gasped and clutched at her chest. Garrick reached for her as she collapsed, saving her from hitting her head on the ground.

"What's wrong?" he asked worriedly.

Her face blanched in terror, then softened into sadness. "Something has happened," she whispered.

"What? What is it?"

"Death, so much death." Her eyes roamed back and forth, as though seeing something other than his face. Her eyes widened.

"Your people," she gasped. "They are in danger!"

"No one loves a warrior until the enemy is at the gate."

—Melchiades

CHAPTER 2

Keswick loomed before Aramis and Melchiades like a mountain.

Gray stone walls, taller than anything Aramis had ever seen, stood vigilant guard around the port city. It was supposedly second in size only to the capital of his kingdom. Judging by the massive stretch of coastal land that the city covered, Aramis wouldn't be surprised if the city of Keswick was larger. Spaced every few yards a guard tower rose from the wall. Aramis wasn't sure, but he thought he could see shrouded figures atop them. A massive portcullis, wide enough to comfortably allow four carriages through side by side, was halfway down.

"That's odd," Aramis said. "Why would the gate be closing so soon?"

Mel shrugged. Exchanging glances, they both urged their mounts to pick up the pace. As they approached the gates, Aramis noticed several heavily armed guards moving to intercept them. Slowing his horse down to a smooth trot, he raised his hand and hailed them.

"What's your business in Keswick?" one of the

guards asked when they stopped.

"We're looking to book passage on a ship."

"Where are you headed?"

Aramis raised his brow, but answered anyway. "Down the coast. Near the Five Islands."

"Oakhaven?" the guard asked.

"Does it matter?" Aramis replied. His patience was beginning to fail and he made it evident in his tone. The guard didn't appear to be bothered by it.

"I'm sorry, sir. Standard procedure. I'm sure you understand?"

"Interrogating people is standard procedure? Since when? Keswick has always been an open city. Has something changed that I'm not aware of?"

The guard pulled his helmet off. Aramis saw the man was young; possibly no older than sixteen winters. A scar ran the length of his face on the left side. The path of mottled flesh barely missed his eye. His hair was black and he had bright blue eyes. Aramis wondered when the boy had been conscripted into the military.

"A lot has changed, I'm afraid. The city has experienced a lot of tragedy recently. The Lady of the city has taken extra precautions to ensure that tragedy stays minimal. I apologize if you feel like I am interrogating you. Unfortunately, the Lady isn't allowing just anyone into the city these days."

Aramis looked past the guard and into the city. It seemed normal. He could see traders in the market offering their wares. People walked about freely. He frowned.

"My friend and I are only looking to book passage on a ship headed for Oakhaven, or anywhere close to it. I've got urgent business there and I cannot delay. Is the harbor still open?"

"Yes, but not for much longer. No ships are permitted to leave port after sundown. If you don't make it onto a ship before then, you can find lodging at one of the inns near the docks. They're older buildings, but fairly priced considering recent events."

"Thank you," Aramis said. "I appreciate the information. You mentioned the Lady of the city. What of her husband? Lord Abriel?"

The young man's face betrayed his emotions long enough for Aramis to deduct that something ill must have happened.

"News doesn't travel well lately," the guard answered solemnly. "Lord Abriel is no longer among the living. Did you know him?"

"Not personally, no. I met him once and we spoke briefly. I'm sorry to hear of his loss. He was a good man."

The guard didn't say anything. Aramis suspected the young man was trying not to cry. *The people of the city must have loved him*, he thought.

"You may want to hurry if you expect to leave the port tonight," the guard finally said.

"Thank you again," Aramis said. The guards moved out of his path. He urged his horse forward and Mel followed him.

They dismounted after entering the city and began looking for a place to leave their horses. Mel spotted a stable to the left and they headed toward it.

"Something bad has happened here," Aramis said quietly. He glanced over at Mel. His friend nodded, but didn't respond. He quickly realized why. The people they passed were eyeing them suspiciously. Some of them even stopped to stare.

"Do you think they recognize me?"

"Let's discuss things somewhere more … private," Mel answered.

"Good idea."

They sold their horses at the stable for a poor price.

The owner told them he had an overabundance of horses and no buyers. He apologized, but didn't seem to care if they were pleased with his offer or not. Aramis accepted the offer, mostly because they didn't need to bring the horses on their journey. It'd cost them a small fortune to ship the animals and their funds were limited.

By the time Aramis and Mel reached the docks, sundown had come and gone. They'd gotten turned around and lost their general sense of direction. Hundreds of people packed the streets and by the time they found someone willing to point them to where they should go, the sky had already darkened. There were a few ships in port, but the area was devoid of any life.

They chose the closest inn to stay at. The sign above the door read *The Compass*. Inside, the place was crowded, hot and loud. Everyone in the place appeared to be a sailor. All the tables were taken so the two squeezed through the mob and made their way to the bar.

"What'll ya have?" the barkeep asked.

"A room for the night would be great," Aramis answered.

"You're in luck. I've got one left. Mostly lads from the sea renting tonight. Two gold for the room. You want anything else?"

"Food," Mel chimed in. "Can you have it delivered to our room?"

The doubtful look on the barkeep's face changed when Mel laid another gold coin on the counter.

"I'll have it up shortly," he said with a toothless grin.

"I appreciate it," Mel answered.

"Room's the last door on the right, second floor."

"Thank you," Aramis said. He led the way through the crowded inn to the stairs and up to their room. Mel paused in the hallway and made sure no one was following them, then stepped into the room and shut the door. It was dark except the moonlight coming from the sole window. Using matches that were on one of the side tables, Mel lit a few candles. The room brightened considerably.

"What do you suppose happened here?" Aramis asked.

"I haven't the faintest idea, my Lord," Mel answered. "It's obvious it was something bad. Particularly so to close a fortified city down at night. Keswick has the largest standing army outside of the capital."

"I know." Aramis walked over to stare out of the window. He could see men lighting the lanterns that lined the cobbled streets below. Other than the distrust of the guards at the gate and some of the people in the streets, the city seemed normal.

"Well, we are stuck here until morning regardless. I say we eat and get some rest. We have plenty to do once we get back to Oakhaven."

Mel nodded in agreement. He could hear footsteps in the hall. A loud knock echoed throughout the room. "That must be the food," Mel said. He opened the door to find a half dozen guards, all armed and armored. They pushed their way into the room. Mel stepped to the side to get out of their way.

"What is the meaning of this?" Aramis demanded.

"Is this them?" one of the guards, the apparent leader, asked.

The guards parted to let a young man come through. Aramis realized it was the scarred young man from the gate. He glanced at Aramis and Mel quickly and then lowered his head. He mumbled something Aramis couldn't hear.

"Speak up," the leader said.

"Yes," the young man answered.

"You're dismissed."

The young man turned to leave and cast a glance

back at Aramis. The look on his face was apologetic. Aramis kept his face as impassive as he could despite his annoyance. There was no telling what sort of trouble was about to ensue.

"I will ask again," Aramis said calmly. "What is the meaning of this?"

"Your presence is requested," the leader finally answered. "If you will." He motioned toward the door.

Aramis looked to Mel. His friend nodded ever so slightly.

"Very well," he said.

The guards escorted them down the stairs, through the crowd, and out of the front door. The streets were mostly empty now; only the occasional drunk passed them. Although there wasn't much light, it was obvious that they were being led toward the direction of the castle. As they turned down various roads, Aramis noticed that some of the buildings were damaged. He had a suspicion that a battle had happened recently.

Roughly a quarter of an hour later, they entered the courtyard of the castle. It was large and open, with gray statues of armored men in various places. As they approached two large doors that led to the inside of the castle, he noticed a large group of guards. They were lined up on either side of the doors and looked uneasy. Several of them kept looking back toward the gatehouse Aramis had just entered through.

Their escort led them into the castle and left them in a small unfurnished room.

"Wait here," the leader said.

Once they were alone, Aramis informed Mel of his observations.

"I noticed the same things," Mel replied. "Perhaps there has been a rebellion?"

"Perhaps," Aramis acknowledged. He ran his hand through his hair and scratched the back of his head. "I can't think of anything else that might have the city on edge, but even that doesn't make sense. Why lock the city down only at night? If there was a rebellion, guards would be walking the streets continuously. I didn't notice additional patrols. The common people are still going about their business as usual."

Before Mel could respond, the door opened and a nicely dressed young man stepped into the room. His clothes were made of expensive materials and by the way he held himself, Aramis figured he was of noble birth.

"Please follow me," the man instructed.

Turning on his heel, he walked out at a quick pace. Aramis and Mel followed him, surprised at the man's stride. They traveled down a long hall and entered a massive dining room. A table, roughly twenty feet long, was covered with dishes of exotic foods. The smells made Aramis's mouth water.

"Smells heavenly," Mel said quietly.

"Mm." Aramis grunted. He expected the man to seat them at the table, but they continued past the table and out of the room into another hall. This one was much shorter and only had one door. The man knocked on the door twice, paused, and then knocked again three times. The door swung open on silent hinges and the young man waved them in.

The first thing Aramis noticed was the bed. It was enormous, with four large posts at each corner that supported a canvas that draped over the entire bed. Incense filled the air, but there was no smoke. The young man bowed, then turned and left the room.

Aramis glanced around. Everything in the room led him to believe this was a bedroom for a noble. Large sturdy pieces of furniture were positioned throughout the room. Expensive combs, bejeweled mirrors and other garish things decorated every available surface. They appeared to be alone in the room. Aramis walked over to a desk that sat in front of a large window. Papers, piled in neat stacks, sat atop the surface.

Perusing them led him to believe they were reports. He saw the word "Warlock" scrawled on many of them. He was about to read one of the reports when a noise drew his attention away. A hidden panel in the wall slid to the side and a woman with two armored guards entered the room.

Aramis had only ever seen Lord Abriel's wife once, but he recognized her immediately. Her beauty was a thing of legend. Despite being in her later years, her beauty still captivated men of all ages. Aramis tore his gaze away from her long enough to see that Mel's mouth was hanging open. Aramis laughed and stepped toward her. One of the guards quickly drew his sword and went into a defensive stance.

"Peace," the woman said.

Gods, thought Aramis, *even her voice is perfect.*

The guard hesitated for a moment, but finally sheathed his weapon.

"My Lady," Aramis greeted. His voice faltered and he had to cough to clear his throat. "My Lady," he said again, bowing.

"Good evening," she replied. "Please, call me Lynessa. I am sorry to have brought you here the way I did, but I didn't see any other option."

"No need to apologize," Aramis managed to say. Words seemed to have fled from his vocabulary. "I must mention that we would have come if you had called upon us."

"I'm sure you would have. Unfortunately, I didn't have time to be proper. You are a wanted criminal. Word of your deeds has reached far. You are fortunate that some of my men recognized you. There are others who would have turned you in already."

"Let me guess," Aramis said as he folded his arms defiantly, "you want me to do something for you or you'll turn me in yourself?"

"You wound me, my Prince. Do you think I am like the beggars, seeking only what I may gain from others? No. I have a petition."

"A petition?" His defiance quickly melted.

"Indeed, but I'm being a terrible host. Are either of you hungry? Or thirsty? I can have a servant fetch something for you?"

"Some wine would be nice," Mel said.

"I agree," Aramis chimed in.

Lynessa grabbed a bell from one of the tables and rang it. Within seconds, a female servant rushed into the room. "Wine for our guests," she said. The servant curtsied and left.

"The matter I'd like to talk about is … delicate. Normally I would host you in the dining room, but I desire privacy in this matter. I'm sure you understand?"

"Of course," Aramis replied.

"Good. I'm not entirely sure how much you know about our recent events, but terrible things have happened."

"I have heard that your husband passed away. I'm sorry to hear that."

"Abriel was murdered," Lynessa said.

Aramis's eyes widened in shock.

"I had debated keeping it a secret from the people. He was loved by everyone, and I didn't want anyone taking rash actions. Before we could deliver the news, something else happened."

The servant returned, bearing a tray with tall glasses. She handed one to Lynessa, then to Aramis and Mel.

"Thank you. You are dismissed for the evening. If I need anything, I'll have one of my guards attend to it."

The servant bowed her head and left. After a few

moments, Lynessa motioned to the door. The guard who had drawn his sword on Aramis left the room and returned a moment later.

"She's gone," he said.

"Very good. I—"

The second guard suddenly threw Lynessa to the ground. Aramis was confused until he saw the glint of steel in his hand. The guard drew his hand back to drive the dagger into her, but the first guard threw himself bodily into the other man. The two rolled around, struggling against one another. Aramis quickly helped Lynessa to her feet and stood protectively in front of her.

One of the men screamed in pain and stopped struggling. The man who tried to kill Lynessa stood up and rushed Aramis. Barely thinking about it, he summoned his armor. The air hissed loudly as the armor formed around him from mist. Just as his armor finished materializing, the man struck him with the dagger. It made a clanging sound as it slid off his breastplate.

Aramis grabbed the man's wrist and twisted it sharply. The man gasped and the blade clattered to the ground. Mel was there suddenly, grabbing the man from behind and locking him in a chokehold. The guard flailed and attempted to fight back, but it was futile. Swiftly rendered unconscious, Mel dropped him to the floor a moment later.

"What is going on?" Aramis said. His pulse was pounding in his head.

"It is as I feared," Lynessa replied. "He has infiltrated my personal guard."

"Who has?"

"The Warlock."

"Who is the Warlock?" Aramis asked.

"Please, we must tend to Cardon first. Can you find one of my servants?"

"I'll go," Mel offered. He hurried off.

Aramis dismissed his armor and knelt beside Cardon. A small pool of blood had formed near the man's shoulder. He gently lifted the man's arm to get a better look. The dagger had pierced him in the armpit and blood was flowing freely from the wound. Aramis ripped the hem of his shirt off and pressed the cloth against the wound. Cardon groaned.

"Will he survive?" Lynessa asked worriedly.

"I've seen men survive much worse. He'll be fine so long as we can stop the bleeding." Aramis was growing worried the longer that Mel was gone. The cloth was already soaked with blood.

"Perhaps I should go find help," Lynessa suggested.

"No," Aramis said immediately. "If your personal guard has been compromised, there's no telling how many of your servants are also assassins in disguise. Mel will get help."

As though hearing his name, Mel came flying into the room with a group of servants trailing him.

"Out of the way!" a deep voice cried out.

An older man pushed his way through the servants and knelt at Cardon's other side. "He's turning pale. Where's the wound?"

"In the armpit," Aramis answered. "I'm trying to halt the blood flow, but it's not going so well."

"Give me your shirt," the older man said. "And get out of the way."

Aramis took it off without hesitation and handed it to the man. The man wrapped the shirt under Cardon's arm and tied a tight knot.

"We've got to take him to the infirmary," he demanded. "Any longer and I can't guarantee he'll live." The servants broke into action. They lifted Cardon and carried him out of the room while the older man shouted orders.

Aramis looked at Lynessa. "Are you all right?" he

asked.

"I'm fine. A little shaken, but I'm fine."

"What should we do about him?" Aramis pointed to the unconscious assassin. "He won't be out forever."

"I'll take care of him," Mel said. He walked over and grabbed the man by his legs, then dragged him out of the room.

Aramis sat down on the floor. His hands were covered in Cardon's blood, so he tried not to touch anything. He realized Lynessa was staring at him.

"So, it's true," she said softly.

"What is?"

"That you bear the mark."

Aramis sighed. "Yes, but it is not what you may think."

"Explain it to me," she said. "My husband was murdered by the Warlock. And he has the same symbol."

Mel entered the room then, followed by more servants. They began cleaning the blood from the floor. One of them began washing Aramis's arms. He tried to protest, but the servant ignored him. Once he was clean, another servant brought him a shirt. It was dark blue and made of a thin material. He put it on and got back on his feet.

After the floor was cleaned, the servants departed. They had done such a good job that Aramis would never have known anyone had almost died.

"May I speak to your prince alone?" Lynessa asked Mel.

He nodded and closed the door behind him as he left.

"Tell me," she said.

Aramis explained everything. As many times as he had told his story, relating his father's death never got easier. After he had related all the details, including his escape from Red Mountain, they sat in silence.

"It sounds like you have suffered as I have suffered," Lynessa finally said. "I trust you."

"It gives my heart gladness to hear it," Aramis replied. "Why did you bring me here?"

"I need your help. The Warlock murdered my husband. I've had the city guard searching for him since it happened, but they have been unsuccessful so far."

"You mentioned something else happened?"

"Yes. I would not have believed it if I had not seen it myself. At night, the dead come alive."

Aramis waited for her to explain. When she didn't, he asked, "What do you mean?"

"There is a graveyard for the nobles not far from here," Lynessa said. "Every night since Abriel's death, the dead rise from their graves and attack the city. I know the Warlock is behind it, but I haven't figured out how."

"You want me to find him."

"If you can. I've heard many rumors concerning you lately. I don't know how much of it is true, but anything you can do would be greatly appreciated."

"I wouldn't know where to start," he said.

"The graveyard will be the best place. I will give you whatever you need. Soldiers, money, anything."

"I would love to assist you, but I'm afraid I can't. There is something much bigger at work and I need to find my father's killer. I can't reclaim my throne if I can't prove I didn't kill my father."

Lynessa closed her eyes and lowered her head, crestfallen. "I had hoped … I don't know what I had hoped," she whispered sadly.

Aramis felt terribly guilty. He considered what she had said. If this Warlock was one of Mordum's agents, it wouldn't hurt to try and track him down. He would certainly need Mel's help, though.

"Lynessa," Aramis said softly, "I will help you."

She lifted her head and met his eyes. He could see tears had started to slide down her face. Even in her sadness, he found her beautiful.

"If you find him, I will reward you with anything you ask. I will publicly swear my loyalty to you as King."

"I will do what I can," Aramis replied.

Lynessa leaned in uncomfortably close to him. He could smell her perfume. Staring into her eyes, he had the sudden urge to kiss her. She must have had the same idea because she moved in even closer. They were mere inches from one another. Pushing his nervousness aside, he was about to kiss her when someone knocked on the door. The interruption broke the moment and Lynessa pulled back.

The door opened and Mel poked his head inside. "You need to see this, my Lord."

"What is it?" Aramis asked, still staring at Lynessa. His heart was thudding against his chest.

"The dead. They're … not dead. They're attacking the city."

CHAPTER 3

Ash.

Jovanna stood on a blackened field. As far as she could see, there was nothing but a smoldering, charred landscape. Scorched bones littered the area. The smell of burnt flesh—and death—filled her nostrils. It was overwhelming. She dropped to her knees and vomited.

Inhale. Exhale.

Jovanna repeated the words in her mind and her body obeyed. She wiped the back of her hand across her lips and spat the vile taste from her mouth. She was stronger than this; *better* than this. She staggered to her feet and immediately felt her strength drain from her. It was all she could do to remain standing. Tremors ran through every muscle in her body. It was a weakness like she had never experienced. A pounding ache in her head reverberated behind her eyes.

The weakness was undeniable, yet she also felt *powerful.* She had done something no one else had. She had used the elven tattoo magic. Her, a human, able to wield both elven magic and human magic. She smiled as the implication slowly came into focus.

She stood and waited for the dizziness to pass. The rushing torrent of magical energy that had left her and caused the destruction that she gazed upon was great indeed, though it left her feeling sick and weak. She would need to learn to control it better.

As her vision returned to normal, Jovanna noticed the elves had regrouped across the field. They were preparing to attack, forming ranks and putting their archers at the rear of their force. She needed to recuperate.

Jovanna tried to turn and retreat to the fortress, but her muscles would not obey her. She stood there, frozen. She was confused. Then she thought maybe one of the elves had cast a spell at her. Closing her eyes, she sent her senses out. Nothing. She could feel the humming of the elves' magical tattoos, but aside from that, there was no other magic in effect.

She opened her eyes and looked down at her legs. They trembled slightly from weakness, but there were no wounds she could see that would keep her from moving. Her confusion turned to anger as she tried harder to move. Had the tattoos she'd inked caused an issue? She watched the magic floating around her calves. Everything seemed normal. Then again, to her knowledge, she was the first human to use the elven magic. Perhaps there was a good reason why humans didn't use it.

The book. She remembered reading in the book that humans had given their elven slaves the tattoos. There was no mention of whether the humans had used them as well. Jovanna sighed in frustration.

A single braying trumpet sounded from the fortress behind her. She turned her head—she had some control—and her eyes widened in shock. The front half of the castle had been blown apart. Had she done that?

The army of elves came across the field at a run, shouting insults and defiance to their foes. Arrows from both sides arced into the skies, forming a canopy of death above the heads of the armies, who came together with a resounding crash. Not far from the fighting, she was trying desperately to move. No one had noticed her. Yet.

Then she saw Garrick, the king of Talvaard, look her way. She had saved his life when the elves were assaulting the walls. Like some fool, she had watched him leap off the castle walls into the midst of the elves, single handedly fighting them off while his men repaired the breach the elves had created.

She watched as combat became hand to hand. The archers on both side were now effectively useless. The two armies were locked together in a bloody embrace. After several moments, she saw the human line of defense break.

Their order and discipline quickly dissolved and chaos ensued. Then, faintly, she felt something in the air. It was magic, she was sure, but it was not like anything she'd experienced before. There was something … *old* to it. She twisted her head in every direction, but she didn't see the source.

Her attention returned to Garrick once she noticed he was fighting one of the elves with the stone skin tattoo. He was fighting a losing battle. She'd helped him once; now he was on his own. And then suddenly, she could move again. Whatever had held her still just dissipated. Jovanna surveyed the battle. There was nothing she could do. Until she learned to control her new magic, everyone was at risk of being killed by anything she cast.

Just as she decided to run, she saw him. His black

robes billowed around him as he stalked through the battlefield. She watched as with barely a touch, he made men collapse to the ground as though they were dead. Her eyes narrowed when she realized it was Tairu.

She unsheathed her sword and ran towards him.

—Adamar

CHAPTER 4

Aramis watched the amassing crowd of corpses from behind the castle's courtyard gates. They shuffled in random directions in what appeared to him to be laziness. Mel stood at his side, a look of disgust on his face. They'd both had their fill of a delicious meal and changed clothes. They were each wearing thin black cloaks over plain brown tunics and black breaches.

Mel had initially scoffed at the plain clothes, but knowing they would likely be covered in blood and the gods knew what else, he had finally acquiesced.

"It's odd," Aramis said. "They don't seem like they are all that dangerous."

"Don't be fooled," one of the nearby guards said. "They only act like that when the Warlock isn't among them. When he is, they become very formidable."

"Formidable would be an understatement," one of the other guards chimed in. "I've fought formidable men before. These things can't die. They're much more than formidable."

"Have either of you seen the Warlock?" Aramis asked.

"No," the first man said.

"I have," said the second. "It was only a glimpse, but that was enough to raise the hackles on my neck. Creepy looking fellow."

"What did he look like?"

"Hard to say," the guard said. "He was wearing a long robe and his face was covered with a hood."

Aramis frowned. "A man in a robe whose features you couldn't see made you uneasy?"

"Of course not," the man bristled. His face flushed with anger. "There's something about his presence that was…" the man grasped at the air as if he could grab ahold of the word he was searching for, "… dark. Evil."

He knew the feeling well. When he'd faced the chimera in the woodland home of the druids, the very air seemed to be sucked from his lungs. The creature's presence was overpowering. Aramis nodded in understanding. He looked around the courtyard and surveyed the demeanor of the guards. Although the gates were closed and barred against the dead, they all seemed anxious. Their hands gripped the hilts of their swords and their eyes darted from shadow to shadow.

"What about the townsfolk?" Aramis asked. "How are they safe outside these walls?"

"The dead act like this normally, so they are safe within their homes or other buildings. The first few nights they came alive was different. They were smarter."

"Smarter?"

"Yes. They knew how to enter buildings, they carried weapons. They had *purpose*. It was as if they had someone commanding them, guiding them to where they should be. I know it sounds odd, but you'd have to have seen it to understand."

Aramis looked to Mel, who only squinted out into the darkness. "What do you think?" Aramis asked. "Should we make our move tonight?"

Mel reached up and tapped his chin with his right hand. "The idea of walking among these disgusting things is appalling." He sighed dramatically. "Yet I suppose the quicker we take action, the quicker we can be done here and move on to our intended destination."

"Agreed," Aramis said. He turned to the guard. "Open the gates."

"What?" The guard looked like he might run off in fear.

"We need to get out there and find the Warlock. Open the gates."

The guard hesitated, looking from the corpses outside the gate to the castle.

"Don't worry," Aramis said. "We won't let any of them breach the wall. We don't even need to open it much, just enough for us to slip out."

Aramis thought the man would deny the request, but he nodded. He waved to the other guard who came over and helped him lift the bar from the gates. Opening the gate just enough to fit his body through, Aramis stepped out among the dead. Mel followed quickly, then pushed the gate back in place. The two guards replaced the bar.

"Good luck," one of them said. "You're going to need it."

"Thanks."

Aramis summoned his blade. The air hissed as the black metaled weapon formed in his hand. Mel did likewise, the silver blade standing in stark contrast to his own. They began making their way through the undead, dodging the corpse's slow-moving attempts to grab at them.

"It's hard to imagine these things actually fighting," Aramis said over his shoulder to Mel.

"I agree, my Lord. The idea that these things could have anything resembling intelligence is … doubtful."

They stopped at the end of the street. It continued straight and forked to the left and to the right. The area was devoid of any of the dead. The street lanterns had been lit and they had plenty of light to see by. The buildings in this area looked similar to the ones they had passed by earlier. Signs of fire, broken windows. Aramis placed the tip of his sword in the cobbled ground and balanced the blade against his leg, then pulled out a piece of parchment.

"This map shows the graveyard should be down the street to our right. A few hundred feet, if that."

"The Lady seems taken with you," Mel said unexpectedly.

"What?" Aramis turned to his friend.

"I can see it in her eyes," Mel added. "She fancies you. She's twice your age, surely, but she likes you. Do you not see it?"

"Oh, I see it," Aramis answered. "She probably would have kissed me if you hadn't walked in earlier."

"If I may be direct, my Lord?"

"You know you can," Aramis said with a laugh. "You've never asked permission before."

"Do not toy with her emotions. If you do not feel the same way about her as you do about Hanna, I would avoid anything other than our current business with her."

At Hanna's name, Aramis pulled the pendant she had given him out from beneath his shirt. It glimmered faintly in the light of the street lanterns. He hadn't thought of Hanna in a while.

"Of course I don't feel the same way," Aramis finally said. "They have two completely different personalities. Lynessa is beautiful and strong. Especially in the wake of her husband's murder. Trying to deal with grief and run a city … I can only imagine what she is going through. Hanna though … Hanna is more than someone whose looks I admire." He placed the pendant back beneath his shirt and rolled the parchment back up. He slipped it into his belt and picked up his sword.

"That's good to hear, my Lord. I fear that her attraction to you may simply be part of her grieving. Freedom changes people."

"Freedom? I wouldn't think the loss of someone beloved to you to be freedom."

"Perhaps freedom was the wrong word. Loneliness, maybe? The lack of love changes people. It makes us do things we would never do otherwise. Certainly, you understand this?"

"Yes," Aramis lied. He knew what Mel meant, of course, but he couldn't say he understood how it *felt*. He didn't like talking about his feelings anyway. "This way," he said. They went to the right and walked for a while in silence. The further they traveled, the less the street lanterns illuminated anything. It was like a dark haze was pulling the light into its depths. Ahead, Aramis saw the small stone wall and steel gate that marked the entryway into the cemetery.

"There," Aramis paused and pointed. "That must be it. It fits the description."

"Something feels wrong here," Mel said.

Aramis looked around them, expecting to see more of the corpses. Everything was quiet. The flame of the lantern to their right flickered sporadically before suddenly dying. They were left in complete darkness except for the pale moonlight that filtered down through the thick murky clouds above. They exchanged glances.

"Eerie," Aramis said. The sound of his voice seemed loud and out of place. Without another word, Aramis headed toward the gate. It swung open on silent hinges. Apparently, it was well kept. Large stepping stones, surrounded by small pebbles, led them into the cemetery.

The footpath was only a few feet wide. On either side of the path, manicured grass stretched out before them. A dense fog blanketed everything. It was so thick Aramis could only see a few feet in any direction.

"This seems like a bad idea," he whispered.

"I couldn't agree more, my Lord," Mel whispered back.

As they continued along the path, they began passing gravesites. Most of them had been disturbed, the grass and dirt having been heaved up off the wooden caskets below the ground. Aramis's senses began to play tricks on him. He thought he saw movement within the shadowy fog, but when he peered toward the movement, there was nothing there. Whispers called out to him, but when he stopped walking, he heard nothing.

"Is it just me, or does this place seem *alive?*" he asked.

"That would be one way to describe it," Mel answered.

The path circled around a large fountain. Gray stone benches were placed on the edges of the pathway, close to the grass. The base of the fountain was round and made of the same gray stone as the benches. An angelic statue stood guard in the center of the fountain, holding a sword in one hand and a shield in the other. Water sprayed mist like into the air from the tip of the blade.

"What is that?" Mel asked.

Aramis turned his attention to where Mel was pointing. A mass of shapes slowly materialized out of the fog. As they came closer, he realized they were corpses. They weren't like those outside of the castle, however. These corpses didn't shuffle around. They walked like normal men and they were armed with swords and axes.

Aramis summoned his armor. He could hear the air hissing around him as Mel did the same. With a sudden quickness, the dead charged them. Aramis brought his sword up in a sweeping arc as one of them came within range. The powerful stroke cut through the creature's rotting flesh easily, but stopped as it struck the dead man's ribcage.

The blow hardly affected the thing. It growled at him and brought its own sword up to strike him. Throwing himself backwards to avoid the blow, he had to let go of his own blade. The dead man came at him, swinging its sword back and forth like an untrained thug. Aramis easily maneuvered himself away from the swings. When he saw an opportunity, he lunged forward and grabbed the hilt of his sword and yanked hard. A cracking noise filled the air and the blade came free. No blood rushed from the wound. He deflected the man's next few strikes and scored a few of his own.

"How do you kill someone who is already dead?" Aramis shouted. He risked a glance over at Mel and saw he was busy fending off two corpses.

"I haven't figured that out yet!" Mel shouted back.

Swinging low, Aramis succeeded in hacking off one of the man's legs. It threatened to fall over, but managed to stay upright. It began hopping toward him. Aramis was unpleasantly surprised to see the limb stand up and reattach itself to the man's stump. It came at him as if nothing had happened.

Gods, he thought, *this was a terrible idea. I don't even know how to fight these things!* Then he thought about Lynessa and her look of disappointment. He couldn't let her down. He wouldn't. With a loud cry, he swung with all his might and removed the dead man's head. The corpse continued to stand for a moment before toppling to the ground. He watched for a moment to see if the thing would get back up. It didn't move.

"Cut off their heads!" he yelled to Mel.

He watched as Mel spun about in a circle and, with

an amazing flourish, both corpses had their heads lopped off.

"You've got company!" Mel shouted.

Aramis turned to find three of the dead men running at him. He growled in frustration and rushed to meet them head on. Though they were obviously untrained, he was outnumbered. He went on the defensive, parrying their strikes. They kept him so busy fending off their attacks that he couldn't get his own strikes in. He began to back pedal, slapping their swords away as he struggled not to trip over himself. His back suddenly slammed into something hard. Glancing back, he saw it was Mel.

His friend was fighting a pair of dead men. Being so focused on the fight, he almost didn't notice the mass of corpses that were joining the fray. It was slow at first. Two and three here or there, but then they started appearing in droves. They were quickly surrounded. Only a small circle of space kept the dead at bay.

Aramis could feel his arms getting heavy. His breathing was getting labored and sweat was dripping down his chest and back. As his defenses began to falter, his armor started taking more hits. Clanging filled the air as the dead men's blows rained down on him. He could hear Mel grunting in pain behind him.

A breeze blew through the cemetery, causing the fog to swirl in random directions. To his right, Aramis caught sight of a small stone building. Two torches were lit on either side of the doorway. He wasn't completely sure, but he thought the door was ajar. And then he had a desperate idea.

"I think I see a defensible position!" he shouted. "We need to clear a path to *my* right. Can you manage it?"

"Yes," Mel answered. The word came out more as a gasp.

Aramis managed the knock the sword out of one of

his attacker's hands, then quickly decapitated him. "Let's go now!"

As one, they turned in the direction of the building and forced their way through the crowd of dead men. Arms and legs got hacked off as the two used the last of their strength to push through the bodies. When they finally broke free, they sprinted to the building and crashed into the stone door. It barely moved. Placing his shoulder against the door, Aramis pushed with all his might. It moved an inch. Mel joined him and they shoved their weight against the door.

With slow momentum, the door finally swung inward. The two men ducked inside and tried to force the door shut. The dead men were quickly closing the distance. Aramis cried out in pain as his muscles threatened to disobey him. He put everything he had into his last shove. The door slid closed with a soft clunk, leaving them in a faintly lit corridor.

Aramis slid down the door, his backside resting on the floor. His exhaustion was complete. There wasn't a muscle in his body that wasn't screaming for relief. Against his better judgement, he dismissed his sword and his armor.

For long moments, the only sound was their heavy breathing. Aramis was burning up. He was soaked with sweat and his clothes clung frustratingly to his flesh. He met Mel's gaze and managed to grin.

"You owe me for this one, my Lord."

Aramis laughed. The absurdity of their situation was obvious. If they could escape the place before daylight, it would be a hard fight all the way back to the castle. If they waited out the night, assuming they survived, they would have to do it all over again the next night.

The air hissed as Mel dismissed his own blade and armor. They sat quietly, each trying to catch their breath and find what rest they could. As their breathing became normal, Aramis thought he could hear something echoing throughout the corridor. It was faint and sounded like singing. He was about to dismiss it as his imagination when Mel looked at him.

"Do you hear that?" he asked.

"I think so," Aramis answered. "It sounds like singing."

"Why would anyone be singing?"

They must have come to the same conclusion at the same time as they both said in unison, "The Warlock."

Aramis pushed himself to his feet and held a hand out to Mel. They locked hands and Aramis leveraged his weight backwards to help Mel onto his feet. They walked cautiously down the corridor, stepping lightly. The hallway ended abruptly with stairs leading down to a lower level. Aramis took the lead and made his way down the stone steps, Mel right behind him. After roughly twenty steps, they found themselves in a small antechamber.

Small spheres of light hovered at random along the room's walls. Old paintings, worn and unrecognizable from time, covered the walls. A once lavish rug, now frayed and faded, decorated the floor. To their left and their right were doorways that lacked any sort of door. Straight ahead, a rotting wooden door hung on rusted hinges.

Glancing through both doorways provided nothing useful. They were dark and from what he could tell, were empty. Aramis could now hear the singing more clearly. But it wasn't singing; it was chanting. It drifted into the chamber from behind the door.

Aramis summoned his blade. He held off on calling his armor. He wanted the element of surprise, and if he entered the room creaking and clanking about, he surely wouldn't have it. Approaching the door, he paused in front of it and listened. The chanting was in a language he did not know. Raising his eyebrows at Mel, he nodded toward the door. Mel shrugged.

Gritting his teeth, Aramis pushed gently on the door. It creaked softly as it partially opened. Cursing the hinges in his mind, he waited. The chanting didn't stop. Not wanting to press his luck, he squeezed himself through the opening. The door creaked again when his shoulder pushed against the door. His anger getting the better of him, he pushed the door completely open. Surprisingly, no sound came from the hinges.

Of course, he fumed.

They entered a large, circular room. Spheres of light, identical to the ones in the previous chamber, illuminated everything with their soft light. The walls and floor were made of marble. The ceiling arched overheard, a dome supported by delicate columns. Embedded in the walls of the room were row after row of glass chambers, chambers intended to hold bodies. Many of them were empty, but others were occupied. From the light of the spheres, Aramis could see aged corpses inside. *A mausoleum,* he realized.

Rows of benches lined the room from left to right. They were separated by a walkway down the middle that led to a raised platform. Upon the platform was a long slab, and in front of that slab stood a robed figure. His back was to them and he was bent over the slab. Aramis inched into the room, treading lightly. Kneeling behind one of the benches, he waved Mel in.

Mel entered the room and knelt behind the row of benches across from Aramis. They watched the figure in silence. Aramis suddenly noticed that atop the slab lay a corpse. The figure continued chanting softly.

"What should we do?" Aramis whispered.

Mel's face scrunched in thought, and after a moment he shrugged.

Aramis looked around the room. Besides the door

they entered, there was only one other located to the right of the platform. The chanting stopped. Aramis froze, not even daring to breathe. The figure left the room. Without having any sort of plan, Aramis sprinted across the room, holding his sword up before him. He stopped just shy of the door and peeked through the doorway. A narrow hallway, roughly fifty feet long, ended abruptly with a stone wall. There were no other doors, yet the figure was nowhere to be seen. He turned to see Mel examining the body on the slab.

"This one is fresh," Mel said softly.

Aramis joined him and looked at the body. He gasped. "That's Lord Abriel. Or, it was."

"Where's the Warlock?" Mel asked, looking toward the doorway.

"I don't know. There's nothing but an empty hallway through there."

Mel frowned. "I don't like this," he said. Then he summoned his armor.

Aramis shuddered. An intense feeling of dread crept up his back and the tattoo on his arm began to burn furiously. The hovering spheres of light were unexpectedly snuffed out, leaving them in darkness. Aramis summoned his armor. The air hissed as it formed.

"I should have known the Lady would send her minions looking for me," a deep voice echoed in the room.

A dull red light broke the darkness. The robed figure stood on the other side of the slab, holding a black wooden staff in his left hand. The light shone from a small crystal on the tip of it. His robes were as black as the staff. A hood was pulled low over the top half of his face. Judging by the lower part, Aramis guessed the man was young.

"I did not expect a fellow follower of Mordum,

however. Are you here with orders? No? I didn't think it likely."

Aramis tried to move, but his muscles wouldn't obey him. His eyes darted to Mel. He seemed frozen as well.

"A neat trick, isn't it? Not when you are on the receiving end of it maybe, but no matter. So, what to do with intruders ..." the man tapped his chin with his index finger. He smiled. "I know."

Leaning down, he began a whispered chant in the corpse's ear. Aramis's skin tingled. The air grew cold, so cold that Aramis could see his breath. Despite the spell the Warlock had cast, he shivered. He could feel the warmth leaving his body. And just as suddenly, the cold was gone.

The Warlock stood back up, the same smile on his face. The body of Lord Abriel began to spasm, here and there at first, but growing in frequency. Abriel's mouth opened and he exhaled loudly. His eyelids opened and Aramis saw nothing but black where the whites of his eyes should have been. Abriel sat up. A wave of foul smelling air hit Aramis's nostrils. The signs of decay had already set in.

"I think I'll leave you two here to get acquainted with the previous lord of the city. I've got people to terrorize and I'd rather not be late."

The Warlock stepped around the slab. "It's a pity the Prophet wants you kept alive," he said to Aramis. "Though there are others who ... don't care as much. Like your brother. Personally, I don't see the resemblance. You can judge for yourself soon enough. Goodbye, gentlemen."

The Warlock faded from sight. As soon as he was gone, the spell of binding ended. Aramis staggered back from the slab. The soulless body of Abriel turned his dead gaze on them. He got off the slab and took shaky steps toward them. Aramis and Mel backed away but took defensive positions.

"I don't know what he's planning, but we've got to stop him," Aramis said.

"I agree, my Lord, but I fear we have troubles of our own now."

Abriel raced toward them, his arms swinging wildly. Aramis threw his sword in an upward arc, cutting off Abriel's left arm at the elbow. That hardly stopped him. He slammed bodily into Aramis and they tumbled to the floor in a mass of blows. Mel jumped in and grabbed Abriel by his tattered shirt and pulled him off Aramis. Pushing Abriel back, Mel brought his own blade across and cut Abriel's head cleanly off his shoulders. The body dropped lifelessly onto the ground.

Mel offered his arm to Aramis and helped him back onto his feet. They stared down at the corpse. Aramis wondered if it was truly that easy. After a few minutes had passed, and the body still hadn't moved, Aramis figured it was safe.

"I don't feel right leaving the body like this," Aramis said.

"What do you mean? What are we supposed to do with it?"

"I think this place is used for putting the city's nobles to rest. I'd hate for someone to come down here and see their previous lord cut to pieces. Let's put him in his ..." he waved to the glass chambers embedded in the walls, "coffin thing."

Mel sighed. "Yes, my Lord."

They found that a small placard with each person's name and house was placed below the chamber that the body rested in. They found Lord Abriel's easy enough as the placard for his name was made of gold. Several minutes of struggling later, they had placed the lord's body, severed arm and head in his chamber and closed the glass paned door.

"Now we must fight our way back to the castle," Aramis said. "Gods, this night just keeps getting better and better."

They backtracked their way to the stone door that sealed the outside world out. No sound could be heard from the other side, so they took the risk of pulling the door open. They were greeted with silence and an empty cemetery.

"Do you think we should get back to the castle?" Mel asked.

"I think that would be a good idea."

They ran the entire way. Aramis fumbled with the map as they ran, navigating them to the correct street. Once they reached the street that led to the castle, Aramis could hear a commotion. They sprinted the remainder of the distance to the gates and found the castle swarming with the dead.

"I bet the Warlock is in there somewhere," Aramis said.

"I know he is," Mel replied, pointing with his sword. The robed man was striding across the courtyard, headed for the castle doors.

"I'll see you inside," Aramis said. Mel nodded to him.

Aramis began cutting his way through the mass of dead, trying to push his way through to the castle. He had to stop the Warlock before he got to Lynessa. Her guards were hard pressed to provide a decent defense. The courtyard was overrun and they were highly outnumbered. Aramis managed to break through the line of dead in time to witness a handful of guards rushing the Warlock.

The Warlock used his staff to block the sword strikes of the guards. He began chanting loudly and waved his hand at the closest guard. The man began screaming and clawing at his own face. Aramis watched in disgust as the man's flesh began melting off his body. The guard dropped dead to the ground a moment later. Aramis tried to close the distance to help the guards.

He was too slow. The Warlock dispatched the other soldiers in a similar fashion and disappeared into the main keep. Aramis growled in frustration. He could feel the power of his tattoo pounding in his body. He denied the temptation to use it.

Entering the keep, he found a scene of chaos and death. Servants and soldiers alike lay dead. Blood was on the walls and the floor. Booted footprints smeared the blood in places. Aramis had to force himself not to vomit. All these innocent people were dead because of Mordum and his servants. Gritting his teeth in anger, he stalked through the room and navigated his way through the confusing halls of the unfamiliar castle.

He encountered a few skirmishes, mostly small groups of soldiers driving the dead back from the inner rooms. Aramis avoided these as much as possible, searching furiously for Lynessa. He managed to find the dining area they had eaten in earlier. After getting turned around a few times, he finally found Lynessa's private chambers. She wasn't present, but the secret door she had emerged from was ajar. Pulling it open, he charged into the darkness.

After a few seconds, his eyes adjusted to the gloom. Torches, too few for adequate light, revealed a narrow corridor. The ceiling was inches above his head and it was only wide enough for one person to pass through at a time. Aramis walked down the hall. He kept his sword up before him, ready for any surprises. The beginning of the corridor was made of stone, but as he continued it became hardened dirt.

"This place was carved into the earth," he muttered to himself.

Ahead, he could see the corridor curved to the left.

He slowed his pace as he approached. He could hear voices. He peeked around the bend. The hall opened into a large room. Several other corridor and stair cases were scattered around the room. Apparently Lynessa had an entire series of secret passages in the castle. As he inched closer, he could see the robed figure of the Warlock. He was standing over someone ... *Lynessa!*

"It seems a pity to kill you," the Warlock said to her. "I could use a queen to help me manage this city. Among other things, of course. Beauty like yours shouldn't be wasted ... but the Prophet was very clear on this matter."

"Please," Lynessa pleaded, "I will give you whatever you want. Please don't kill me."

"As enticing as that sounds, I'm afraid it won't do you any good. If I want something, I take it. Your husband's life, your city, and now ... your throne."

"Not if I can help it," Aramis said as he entered the chamber.

"Aramis!" Lynessa screamed in relief.

"The exiled prince," the Warlock said with a tone of boredom.

"I'm not as easy to kill as you presume," Aramis said.

"I wasn't trying to kill you," the Warlock replied with a laugh. "I was merely trying to slow you down. How did it feel, anyway?"

"How did what feel?" Aramis asked, spinning and twisting his sword around in front of him. He was ready to end this already.

"Why, cutting up the lord of the city. Did you know that he was down in the mausoleum?" the Warlock asked Lynessa. "He went down there to desecrate your dead husband's body."

Lynessa looked at Aramis with uncertainty. Aramis glared at the Warlock.

"You know that's a lie," Aramis said. "Stop talking and fight me."

"Fight you?" the Warlock asked as he pulled the hood of his robe back. Aramis had been right. The man *was* young, perhaps only a few years younger than himself. The Warlock set his staff on the ground and removed his robe. The staff remained standing upright and the Warlock placed his robe on it. He wore black leather boots, black breaches, and a loose fitting black tunic with no sleeves on. He took a few steps toward Aramis with his arms outstretched. Aramis could see the mark of Mordum on his forearm.

"I fear that what is about to happen will not be so much of a fight as it will be a slaughter." The Warlock laughed maniacally.

"Tough words," Aramis said. "Prove them with your actions."

"Fair enough." The air hissed as armor formed around the Warlock from mist. A wicked looking blade formed in his hand. It was completely different than Aramis's own blade.

They stood staring at each other in silence. Aramis was confident he could take the Warlock if their fight was only with blades. If the man used magic, he'd be at a sore disadvantage. He glanced to Lynessa. She was sitting on the ground with her knees pulled up against her chest. Even dirty and forlorn she was breathtaking.

The Warlock came at him in a blinding rush. Aramis forced his attention to the man and brought his sword up defensively. As their swords clashed, a multitude of black sparks filled the air and their blades disappeared with a loud hum. They staggered back from each other in confusion. Aramis tried to summon his blade back, but nothing happened. He still had his armor. That was something, at least.

"Mordum certainly has a sense of humor," the

Warlock said. "Looks like we must settle this with magic."

Aramis cursed the god of death in his mind. Feeling for the power of his tattoo, he was surprised to find it was gone. Frantic with fear, he focused all his willpower into finding the power. He could feel it, barely. There was some sort of barrier around the power. When he tried to grab at it with his will, it slipped away from him.

"Having trouble?" the Warlock cackled. "This will be fun."

An intense, searing pain erupted in Aramis's torso. He gasped and collapsed to his knees, clutching at his chest. His breath came in short wheezes. His body shuddered from the pain. Any thought of trying to summon his power quickly fled his mind. The burning sensation spread down from his chest into his stomach, all the way down to his legs. His body jerked involuntarily with spasms. He thought he could hear laughing. In the chaos, a voice spoke to him inside his mind. It was somehow familiar to him. It broke through the pain enough for him to understand it.

Focus.

I can't, his mind groaned.

Focus! Pierce the veil that hides your power.

How?

Focus.

And then the voice was gone. Aramis writhed in agony. In the haze of his vision, he could see the Warlock moving toward Lynessa. Tears of pain filled his eyes and he knew in that moment he was going to fail her. She would die while he laid there powerless. He clenched his eyes shut. He couldn't bear to watch.

There, in the darkness of his mind, something flashed. Something small, but sharp. It was silver and triangular, like the tip of an arrow. *The tip of an arrow.* Aramis grasped desperately at it, trying to pull himself away from the pain. Clutching it with everything he had, he drove it into the slippery wall around his flow of power.

A small crack.

He stabbed the wall again. The crack, almost imperceptibly, widened. Striking the weakness repeatedly, he could feel it growing larger. It became like a spider web, branching out in every direction. The searing pain threatened to break his concentration. He drove the edge as hard as he could into the crevice.

The wall threatened to collapse. The power of Mordum began to flow through the gap. Slowly at first, but then it began to pour through. It rushed through the wall, tearing it apart. The power invigorated him. Aramis breathed in deep. The searing pain was suddenly snuffed out by the power. Regaining control of his body, he opened his eyes and saw the Warlock strike Lynessa in the head with his staff.

"No!" he screamed. He reached toward the Warlock and the power flowed from his hand. It was like a thick, black river flowing through the air. It struck the Warlock in the back, flinging him forward. He crashed into the wall with a groan.

Aramis stood up. He had never felt the power so strongly, so *powerfully*. His arms began to tremble. It threatened to overtake his willpower. He forced himself to control it, to bend the power to his will. It took tremendous effort, but he managed to keep it in check. The Warlock got up and staggered toward him. Aramis crafted a shield of power and kept the Warlock at bay.

The power wanted him to drain the Warlock. Faint wavering colors danced around the man. The colors jerked away from his shield as if in fear. Somehow, Aramis knew the colors were the Warlock's soul. With one hand, he reached out and grabbed one of the waves of color. He gripped it tightly and the Warlock cried out in agony. In a quick, sudden movement he yanked the color.

Blood began flowing freely from the Warlock's nostrils. He coughed several times and bloody spittle flew forth from his mouth. The knowledge that he was killing the Warlock suddenly revealed itself to him. A sinister smile crept onto his face. This was power! This was what it was like to have endless power at your disposal.

Aramis drew near to the Warlock. He sent a powerful kick into the Warlock's knee. With a snapping noise, the Warlock dropped to the ground. The lower part of the man's face was covered in blood. He smiled up at Aramis, but not in defiance. Aramis wanted to crush the life from him.

"Welcome … to … m-madness," the Warlock uttered softly, still smiling.

The words immediately sobered him. Aramis stared around in confusion, not realizing what he was doing. He saw Lynessa lying a few feet away. The Warlock lay at his feet, choking and laughing at the same time. He dismissed his armor and pulled the rusty dagger from his belt. Kneeling besides the Warlock, he held the blade over the man's neck.

"Madness," the Warlock uttered again. He repeated it over and over between his coughs. The word sent chills down Aramis's spine. With a suddenness that surprised himself, he cut the Warlock's throat. Blood spurted from the wound immediately and the Warlock jerked. Aramis watched as the life slowly left the man, then he closed the Warlock's eyes.

He took a few steps toward Lynessa's still form. An intense weakness overcame him and he staggered briefly before collapsing to the ground. The last thing in his mind before unconsciousness took him was how cold the floor was.

CHAPTER 5

Garrick drove his horse as fast as it would carry him, pushing it to its limit. The landscape whirled by him in a flash. Whatever Laracova had seen, it was terrible enough to urge him to leave immediately. She'd promised her priests would follow quickly. Kelvin had used his power, after knocking him unconscious again, to take him as close as possible to the fortress they'd set out from.

Not knowing what awaited him, he rushed to get there quickly. His people were in danger, she had said. He knew it had something to do with the elves. Had they breached the walls again? He could only guess. The horse was foaming at the mouth. He'd found the beast roaming freely with no rider, yet saddled and ready for battle. It hadn't shied away when he'd approached it. And so, he took it.

As the fortress came into view, he could see smoke rising into the sky. He fought to push the fear down, to keep a clear mind. The distance felt like an eternity as the horse's pace began to slow. After a quarter of an hour, the horse finally stopped altogether and collapsed. He didn't have time to worry about the beast. He sprinted onward, closing the distance.

The nearer he got, the more the damage became apparent. Where there had once been grass was only ash. Bodies littered the area, some of them still smoking. A trumpet sounded. Whether from his fortress or from the elves, he couldn't tell. Sweat drenched his clothes. He slowed his pace as he rounded the side of the fortress. Garrick came to a dead stop when he saw the extent of the damage. The front section of the wall was gone. There were no signs of siege machines. No loose stones to show that it had been knocked down. The entire wall was simply missing.

Scattered cries echoed from the men inside the fortress. Across the way, at the edge of the blackened landscape, a large force of elves dashed across the open field. With the fortress now open to them, the men had little chance of fending them off. He noticed someone standing in the field. From the distance, he didn't recognize who it was.

Another trumpet sounded. Waves of men poured out of the ruined fortress, forming ranks across the open gap. Swordsmen grouped together in tight knit squads and archers lined up behind them. Garrick's heart swelled with pride as he witnessed the product of their training. He summoned his armor and his blade and ran to join them.

He recognized Rycroft's voice shouting orders and directing the men. Garrick changed direction and headed toward his general.

"What happened?" he asked as he neared the man.

Rycroft's face brightened in surprise. "My King!" He bowed low.

"Quickly! What happened here?" Garrick repeated.

Rycroft pointed toward the lone figure out in the field. "She happened. It's the girl that helped you when the elves broke through the wall. I don't know what she did, but she used magic and … this," he waved at the devastation. Garrick frowned. *She caused all this,* he thought.

"Hold your positions!" Rycroft shouted.

Garrick saw the elves were advancing quickly. They didn't have time to talk. He nodded to his general, then took a position next to a group of soldiers. He pulled his helm down and prepared himself. The seconds felt like eternity as they passed. His adrenaline began surging as the first of the elves met their line. A war cry went up as a chorus from the elves and more trumpets blared.

The two forces met in clattering press of shields and a ringing of swords. The sounds of metal impacting metal were punctuated by shouts of challenge and screams of agony. Here and there, explosions sounded and the ground shook as the elves unleashed their devastating magic.

Garrick kept his gaze straight ahead, studying his enemy as they came rushing at him. He ignored the chaos around him as their defensive line shattered. Soldiers abandoned their formations, behaving as individuals instead of a unit.

Two soldiers veered toward him. He used his body as a shield against the first, feeling the force of the elf crash into his armor. His armor protected him and caused the elf to go flying backwards as he struck Garrick head on. The second elf fell to his blade quickly. Garrick stabbed his blade into the neck of the first elf as he stepped over the shocked warrior.

Another elf wielding a longsword swung at him. Garrick parried the elf's blade with the flat of his own sword, so ferociously that the elf wavered in his stance.

Pressing his advantage, Garrick braced himself and swung his sword into the elf's head. A wave of blood and gore washed over him as the blade sheared through flesh and bone, cleaving half of the elf's face off.

Garrick plunged his sword into another elf, piercing his thin armor. The elf screamed. Garrick kicked the warrior, then turned to face another elf. The sounds of battle filled the air, making it hard to hear any one sound over another. Screams of the dying, the clash of steel, and magical explosions were everywhere. Garrick fought with all he had, knowing that if the elves breached their line and reached the ruined fortress, their main line of defense against an invasion would be broken.

He swung his sword at another elf, but his blade bounced harmlessly off the elf's skin. Garrick cursed, remembering the last time he encountered one of the stone skinned elves. The only way he knew to overpower them involved magic, and he was no wizard. He risked a glance to Jovanna, the woman who had found a way to defeat the elven magic. He needed her help.

He launched himself into a furious offensive, hoping to push the elf close enough to the woman to get her assistance. He scored several hits that would have killed anyone else. The elf's skin turned his blade aside every time. Since the elf had no concern for his safety, his plan quickly crumbled. The elf pressed his own attack, driving Garrick back towards the failing line of defense.

Three more elves joined the fray. Not only was he now outnumbered, he also couldn't kill half of his enemies. He focused his attention on the two elves who did not have the stone skin spell. He took several blows from the other two, but he had to slim their advantage. Garrick managed to cut one across the stomach, spilling his blood and organs. The other elf seemed to be more trained in battle and put up a better fight.

Garrick cursed in frustration. He knew they were losing. He stepped over more of his own men's bodies than he did those of elves as he back peddled from their attacks.

A trumpet split the air. Garrick couldn't turn his attention away from his enemy. He was on the defensive, mostly trying to keep from getting struck. He caught a flash of silver in his peripheral. Then another. His enemies halted their attack long enough for him to turn and see that Zevea's priests were beginning to arrive. The air pulsed in random spots as their forms magically appeared on the battlefield. As soon as they became visible, the priests charged toward the elves, bolstering the line.

The sight of added numbers, priests with magical armor and blades no less, gave Garrick hope that they could turn the tide. He amped up the energy of his attacks, throwing himself bodily into the elves to drive them back. He managed to force them where he wanted, but realized Jovanna was gone. Garrick twisted his head left and right, trying to spot her. She appeared to have vanished.

His only advantage gone, he gave up the fight and ran, trying to put distance between himself and the stone skin elves. Garrick noticed that Zevea's priests also had trouble fighting them. Despite wielding god-blessed weapons, they were useless against the elven magic.

The line was holding now. Garrick saw the soldiers regrouping. The archers, protected by the line of swordsmen, were firing arrows over their heads and into the elven ranks. It was working for now, but if they couldn't find a way to kill the stone skinned elves, they would quickly lose the stalemate.

And then something caught Garrick's attention. A black robed elf. He stood amidst the battle, unperturbed by anything happening around him. He walked along the bloody field, touching human soldiers as he passed by them. The men crumbled to the ground, writhing in agony.

Garrick grit his teeth and stalked toward him. As he closed in on the dangerous elf, he saw something else that shook his faith. When the elf raised his arm to touch another soldier, the sleeve of his robes fell back to reveal an upside down black cross. The Mark of Mordum. Confusion, then anger, filled him.

Why was Mordum leading an attack against one of his own followers?

He charged the elf, raising his blade and attempting to strike him down in one blow. His aim was off, though he didn't know how. His sword glanced off the elf's robe. It was like striking a shield. For the hundredth time, Garrick cursed the elven magic.

The elf pointed at Garrick with one hand and touched one of his tattoos with the other. A great gout of flames rushed through the air towards him. Garrick could feel the heat before the conflagration reached him. He dove out of the way, rolling and coming back up onto his feet. The two stared at each other.

"What are you doing here?" Garrick demanded. "We are both servants of Mordum."

The elf pulled his hood back and smiled. "I'm not here for Mordum's cause," the elf answered. "I'm here for my own." The elf touched another tattoo and a jagged fork of white lightning zig zagged towards him.

Garrick lifted his blade up and deflected the bolt into the sky. He knew the elf held the advantage. Aside from whatever gift Mordum had given the elf, he also had the tattoo magic. Garrick decided then that he needed wizards of his own.

The two circled one another. Garrick leapt into the air, raised his sword up and swung down hard. The elf lifted his arms up in an "X" shape, blocking the blade.

Garrick scurried back in case the elf decided to launch his own attack and saw that while he had not struck a mortal wound, the elf's forearms were bleeding. That gave him hope that his enemy could be killed.

Suddenly, Garrick felt his feet leave the ground. He flew backwards a short distance and crashed to the ground on his back. He struggled to rise as he watched the elf come closer. A glow surrounded the elf and he raised his arm up. Garrick saw a flickering orb swirling in the palm of the elf's hand. Garrick flinched as the magical ball suddenly grew blindingly brighter.

From his peripheral, he saw a shadow rush by. Jovanna knocked the elf's arm aside as he released the magic. The radiant globe struck the ground a few feet away from Garrick. The concussive force shook the ground and rattled Garrick's armor.

Tairu's face was locked in a look of disbelief. Jovanna swung her sword at him, attempting to strike the elf in the chest. The blade deflected at the last moment, and Jovanna could feel the magic of the spell that protected him as it flared to life.

She summoned her own magic. It flooded her senses and she almost lost control of it again. At the last second, she forced her will on the flow of energy and cast a shower of fiery darts at him with a wave of her hand. They fizzled out of existence as they neared him. She was impressed. His magic was strong.

Jovanna staggered back as Tairu cast his own spell at her. A wave of cold air swept toward her, freezing everything it touched with tiny crystals. She summoned a shield of flame in front of her. The two elements crackled with bright flashes as the spells negated one another.

Garrick stood up and began circling around Tairu, hoping to flank him. The elf saw him and turned himself at an angle so that he was facing both of his enemies.

"Surrender," Garrick demanded. "You can't hope to win this battle."

Tairu laughed, but his gaze didn't waver from Jovanna. "I don't need to win. I have already set events in motion that cannot be stopped. Even if I fall in battle, my cause will carry on."

The air flashed and crackled as Jovanna and Tairu threw spells at one another. Garrick had to shield his eyes with his arm to keep from being blinded.

"I can feel your strength," Tairu said to her as their magical barrage faded. "The tattoos enhance it, but you are strong without them. Why are wasting your talent with *them*?" he sneered. "Join my cause and no one can stop us."

"Enough talk," Jovanna growled. She jabbed her blade toward him. Tairu backed up out of her range.

"As you wish," he mocked with a bow. "Let's end this!"

A harsh wind picked up as he summoned the magic of every tattoo on his body. All of the symbols burst into life, glowing a faint blue.

Garrick could feel the air humming. The ground around the elf split with small cracks. Not sure if his armor could protect him from what was about to happen, he sprinted towards the castle. *Let the wizards duel it out,* he thought. *I'll fight flesh and blood.*

Jovanna channeled the magic around her into a spherical barrier. She doubted it would hold up against the onslaught, but anything that could help her get close enough to him would be better than nothing at all.

Tairu released his magic. Streaks of red fire, bolts of blue lightning, and many other magical attacks that Jovanna couldn't name struck her shield. Her strength quickly faded and the barrier flickered, almost dissipating completely. She fought to keep the shield up as the attacks crashed into it.

For a split second, a thin veil of space amidst the magical bombardment opened. She glimpsed the magic that fueled Tairu's spells, a rushing torrent of energy that churned around him. She seized the opportunity. Closing her eyes, she envisioned the flow of magic and threw everything she had at it, trying to form a barricade around the elf.

Jovanna could feel the darkness of unconsciousness clawing for her. As the magic howled around them, she unwillingly dropped to her knees. The magic whirling around Tairu began to slow. She could sense him fighting against her, trying to battle her will with his own.

She felt the magic pulse once and opened her eyes. The magic blinded her and tears stung her eyes, running freely down her cheeks. A blazing white light was all she could see as the magic shuddered, flared and with a roar, shattered and exploded into a thousand fragments. An inhuman shriek tore from Tairu's throat and the elf burst into flame.

Jovanna collapsed onto the ground.

Dying wasn't at all like she thought it would be. It felt more like being sleepy. The absence of fear, pain and regret was comforting.

I will assist you, a voice in her mind said.

Jovanna briefly felt magic, old and powerful. And then the last of her strength faltered and everything went black.

—Prince Aramis

CHAPTER 6

He walked along a desolate road that wound its way through a dead valley. The dry grass, yellows and browns, crunched beneath his feet. In the distance, smoke rose lazily into the sky. He didn't know where he was; he only knew he had to get somewhere he couldn't remember.

He felt nothing. His muscles did not tire; his skin did not sweat; he was neither hot nor cold. He walked for what seemed like days, though he could not tell the passage of time. He did not see a sun or a moon in the sky, though the atmosphere seemed to always be illuminated.

After an eternity, he drew close to the source of the smoke. An abandoned town. Most the buildings were blackened husks. The smoke was filtering up into the air from the chimney of the only intact building. He walked to the building and paused at the doors. The place appeared to be a temple. He felt drawn to it. This was the place he needed to be.

He pushed the door open and stepped inside. It was dark. A few scattered lanterns, all of them sputtering into death, provided a dim flickering glow. Several empty tables and chairs filled the room. In the far corner of the room, one table was occupied. A figure was sitting in the shadows. He walked to the table and stood before it.

"I knew you would come," a female voice said. He didn't recognize it.

"Why am I here?" he asked.

"You are broken," the voice answered.

"I don't understand."

"There are many who don't."

He paused. The answers were cryptic and confusing. "Please explain."

The woman laughed. "They are all impatient like you. You are broken. Your mind has been severed. It happens to most of you."

"Most of who?" he asked.

"The servants."

"What servants?"

"My, my. You are a bit slower than the others. The servants of Mordum."

"I'm not one of them," he said.

"Do you bear the mark? Do you summon the blade and the armor? Do you call upon the power that flows from the mark? Then yes, you are one of them."

That made his stomach lurch. "I use the tools for my own means. That doesn't mean I obey him."

"You are here, aren't you? Only those Mordum commands can come to this place."

He looked around the room. There was nothing to indicate the place was different from anywhere else. "Where am I?"

"You are here."

"Where is 'here'?"

The woman leaned forward into the light and smiled. "You are in the place between life and death."

"I'm dead?" he asked, panicked.

"Not quite. Mordum doesn't let his servants out that easy."

"So, I'm alive, then?"

The woman pursed her lips. "That's not quite true either. You are in the middle of the two, dangling precariously. Only the strong make it out of here, if that's what you want to call it."

"What do you mean?"

"Once you've been here, you're never the same."

"How so?"

"Do I look like a sage? I cannot give you all of the answers."

"Who are you?" he asked.

"I'm a sentinel. I guard the path to death."

"How do I get out of here?"

"Through the door you entered."

"No, I meant—" he sighed. "How do I get out of this place? Not this building. This place between life and death?"

"You have to die."

"What? You said only the strong get out."

"I did. Death is not for the weak. It is for the strong. Death brings clarity. Power. Wisdom. And ... madness. Most cannot handle it."

"I've heard that before," he said. When he tried to remember where, his thoughts grew muddled.

"I'm sure you have."

"Someone said it. I-I can't remember who." He shook his head as if that would help clear his mind.

"Be that as it may. It's not important." The woman stood up and came around the table. She was shorter

than he was. Her face was one that time had aged beyond years. She wasn't ugly, but she wasn't attractive either. When he looked into her eyes, he saw nothing but his own reflection.

"Brace yourself," she said. "This is going to hurt."

By the time he realized she was holding a dagger, she had already plunged it into his chest. He expected there to be pain, but there was nothing. She hesitated, then she pulled the blade out and stabbed him again. Still, there was nothing. They stood there for a moment before she finally pulled the blade out.

"Interesting," she said.

"What is?" he asked.

"Apparently Mordum has ... different plans for you." She sheathed the blade at her hip. She stepped closer to him and kissed him. It was a deep, passionate kiss. He was so taken aback, he merely let it happen. As he regained his wits and tried to pull away, he couldn't. And then she began to blow into his mouth.

The air was heavy and began to choke him. He fought to push her away, but they were locked together at the lips. In her eyes, he saw himself struggling. He saw a shadow pass between them. His vision darkened and his strength failed him. And then he was falling. He fell through the floor and into darkness.

● ∞ ● ∞ ●

Aramis opened his eyes. He was lying in a bed, an extremely comfortable bed. He sat up and rubbed his bleary eyes. He groaned. Every muscle in his body ached. He felt as though he'd been struck with hundreds of stones.

"You're awake."

The voice startled him. He looked around confusedly. A veil covered the bed. He could make out the shape of someone, but he couldn't tell who it was. The veil parted and Lynessa peeked in.

"Lynessa? What ... where am I?"

"You are in my personal chambers," she replied.

"What happened?"

"You killed the Warlock. You must have passed out. When I came to, you were out cold and the Warlock was dead, his throat slit. I called for my guards and had them bring you up here."

Aramis rubbed the side of his face. The thin stubble of hair was prickly against his hand. A dull ache pounded at the base of his neck. He'd killed the Warlock? The haziness of his thoughts blotted out all the details, but he did remember bits and pieces. He'd used his dagger to cut the man's throat. He'd saved Lynessa's life. Relief flooded him.

"What about Mel? Is he ..."

"He's fine," Lynessa said. "He refused to leave your side. It took a few hours, but I finally convinced him to leave. I told him I would watch over you as well as he would."

Aramis chuckled. "He's very devoted."

"That's an understatement. He's loyal to the core of his being. His loyalty is not blind, though. Nor is it forced. His loyalty is a sincere bond pledged out of respect and gratitude. That says a lot about his character, but it speaks volumes more about yours."

Aramis shook his head. "I'm no different than anyone else."

"That's not true. You risked your life for my people. And for me." She pushed through the veil and climbed onto the bed. "You saved my city. You saved *me*." She crawled to him on all four. Aramis was suddenly aware that she was only wearing a very thin robe, so sheer as to be transparent. His face flushed and he looked away. She pushed him down and straddled him.

"Lynessa, I—"

"Shh," she said as she placed her finger on his lips. "You are a hero, Aramis. Now enjoy your reward."

● ∞ ● ∞ ●

The next morning, Aramis awoke feeling refreshed and well rested. The silk sheets felt good against his bare skin. He rolled over to find that Lynessa was gone. He sat up and tried to peer through the veil. As far as he could tell, there was no one in the room. He felt around under the sheets for his clothes but couldn't find them.

Aramis rolled out of the bed. Atop a side table, a neatly stacked pile of clothes was laid out. His boots had been cleaned and polished and set next to the clothes. As he finished getting dressed, he heard a soft knock at the door.

"Come in," he said. He slid his boots on and ran his hands through his hair. The door opened to reveal a servant.

"My Lord," he greeted formally, bowing at the waist. "My Lady asked me to deliver this to you."

The servant entered the room and handed him a letter. "She's asked that you not read it until you've left the city."

Aramis raised his brow in question, but the servant either didn't notice or didn't know what to say. Aramis tucked the letter into his belt. "Thank you. I'd like to have a letter sent to the Lady. Can you do that for me?"

The servant nodded. "I'll get the items you need. I'll return shortly, my Lord."

After the man left, Aramis found a tall mirror on one of the walls and checked his appearance. *I need to shave,* he thought. Whoever had picked the clothes he'd been given had a good fashion sense. He was wearing a dark green tunic and a pair of brown trousers.

"My King." Mel's familiar voice greeted him. Aramis turned from the mirror to see his friend standing in the doorway. "I'm glad to see you are well."

"I'm fine," Aramis said with a smile. "I heard you wouldn't leave my side."

"I never will," Mel said.

The servant returned with a parchment, an ink jar and a quill. He laid them on a table and sat down. Aramis turned his thoughts to the words he wanted to leave with Lynessa. He knew what he wanted to ask her. He cleared his throat and dictated the letter to the servant. When he finished, the servant sealed the letter.

"Please make sure she gets this," Aramis said in a serious tone. The servant bowed and left. Aramis checked himself in the mirror one more time. "We should be able to book a ship now," he said. "I'm sure Lynessa has lifted the city restrictions. Hopefully the people here can return to some semblance of normal life."

"Most of the corpses have been moved back to the cemetery," Mel said. "What happened down there, anyway?"

"I'm not sure," Aramis replied. "It's all a haze. The only thing I clearly remember is killing the Warlock."

Mel stepped in close. "It was foolish for you to attack him alone. He could have—" Mel stopped short.

"Could have what?" Aramis asked.

"What's wrong with your eyes?" Mel asked, changing the subject and peering closely.

"What do you mean?"

"They look black. Not noticeably, but ... I can see a change."

Aramis frowned and looked back in the mirror. He didn't know what Mel was talking about. There was nothing wrong with his ...

Mel was right. It was faint, but there was a black

tinge to the whites of his eyes. "*Gods*," he breathed. "What is that?"

"I'm afraid I don't know, my Lord." Mel frowned.

"Well, it's not obvious. Hopefully it doesn't get worse. Come," he led Mel out of the bedchamber. "We've got to find a ship."

"Rarely is a situation forced upon us. Be aware of your power to choose and take responsibility for what you allow to happen."

—General Garrick

CHAPTER 7

Aramis and Mel found a ship heading down the coast and booked passage for a reasonable price. After several minutes of Mel complaining about not getting the food they had paid for, they returned to *The Compass*. The barkeep from the previous night was there preparing for the day's business. He paused in his work upon seeing them.

"I don't much mind ruffians in here, but I won't stand for trouble from anyone that's been escorted out by the Lady's guard."

"I completely understand," Aramis replied. "Though I think there may be some confusion. We were summoned to the Lady for a task, not because we are in trouble."

The older man eyed they warily. "What d'ye need then?"

"We paid for a room and food," Mel chimed in. "And as you are aware, we didn't receive either."

The barkeep glared at them and pointed above the bar. Aramis noticed a sign that read: *No Restitution*.

"I see," Aramis said. "Perhaps I can explain what happened?"

"I'm sure that ye can," the man said, "though ye won't find an audience." With that, the man stomped off behind the bar and disappeared through a door.

"Well," Mel huffed, "I don't think I've received such horrible treatment before in my entire life."

"You exaggerate. You were killed by a templar, remember?"

"Don't remind me," Mel said.

They turned to leave and found the way blocked by one of the city guards. "What now?" Mel muttered.

The guard stepped into the inn and removed his helm. It was the scarred young man from the gate. He knelt at Aramis's feet and bowed his head.

"Please, rise," Aramis said.

The man stood up. "I want to apologize for squealing."

"There's no need," Aramis replied.

"I feel like I betrayed you somehow."

"Nonsense. You were following orders. I respect that."

"Even so, you are my king. I should have warned you, at least."

"You are forgiven of whatever you believe you did wrong," Aramis said. "Are you on duty?"

"No, sir. Well, not on guard duty. I work here with my father in my off time."

"You should talk him into changing his policy," Mel said, nodding to the sign over the bar.

The youth rolled his eyes. "He's a stubborn one. What does he owe you?"

"Don't worry about it," Aramis said. He gave Mel a look.

"Can I get you anything before you leave? I assume you are sailing out today now that the port is open?"

"Yes, we leave within the hour. Some breakfast wouldn't be too much, would it?"

"Of course not," the youth said. With a grin, he walked to the back of the inn. "Have a seat," he called back at them.

Shrugging, Aramis picked a random table and made himself comfortable. Mel sat across from him. They stared at one another in silence. The youth came back a few minutes later with two plates of food. He set them down, then went back to the bar and returned with two mugs of ale.

"You want anything else?" he asked.

"No, this is perfect. What's your name?" Aramis asked.

"Jarrod."

"You obviously know me. This is my friend Melchiades. I call him Mel."

"It's an honor," Jarrod said. "I've never met a king before. Do you mind if I sit with you?"

"By all means," Aramis said between mouthfuls of food.

"What brings you all the way to Keswick?"

"We need to take a ship back to Oakhaven."

"I know that. I mean, what are you doing so far from your castle? Oakhaven is hundreds of miles from here. What brings you so far from home?"

Aramis and Mel exchanged glances. "It's a long story," Aramis replied. "I don't think we have enough time for me to tell it in full."

"I heard about the king, your father. I'm sorry to hear what happened."

"Thank you. I have been searching for my father's killer. That's what has brought me out here. Have you heard of Red Mountain?"

Jarrod scrunched his eyes as if trying to remember something. "Possibly," he said after a moment.

"It's in the Deadlands. There is a wizard there who was guarding something I needed. That's where we were before we came here to Keswick."

Jarrod's face lit up in excitement. "You went to see an elven wizard?"

Aramis shook his head. "No. She was a human wizard."

"Is she dead?"

"No," Aramis said, taken aback. "Why?"

"You said she *was* a human wizard. I just thought …"

Aramis nodded. "Ah, yes. No, she is not dead. If not for her, Mel and I might have been."

"What happened?" Jarrod asked.

Aramis looked to the bar and eyed the hourglass. "We might have enough time. I had arrived at Red Mountain …"

● ∞ ● ∞ ●

"Mel?" Aramis asked. *I must be dead,* he thought. The smell of charred flesh assailed him. The dead Lamias were unrecognizable except for their tails, some of which writhed among the ashes. Mel reached out his hand, offering his assistance. Aramis accepted it hesitantly, still unbelieving.

"Hurry, my Lord. We don't have much time."

"How?" Aramis asked.

"I'll explain later. Come." Mel pulled Aramis to his feet.

Aramis grunted. His entire body was sore. He eyed himself and saw that his armor had cracks in various places. He wondered if he had struck his head on the ground. Certainly, Mel couldn't be here. How could he be? How would he have gotten inside of the Nexus?

Mel led the way through the maze of corridors. There didn't appear to be any pattern to his navigation. "Do you know where you are going?" he asked.

"I do," Mel answered. "My goddess has shown me the way."

"Did Edria bring you back from the dead as well?"

Mel stopped walking and turned to face him. "No. Edria is …" Mel's face slackened in sadness.

"What is it?"

"Edria is dead."

Aramis was confused. "How is your goddess dead? Aren't gods immortal?"

"It would appear that is not the case."

"How did she die?"

Mel swallowed hard, the struggle not to cry evident on his face. "Mordum killed her."

Aramis was stunned into silence. Things were more serious than he'd thought. Mel turned and resumed his pace.

"I faced the templar, but I was outmatched. I've never feared death until that moment. When he struck me a killing blow, I thought I had failed you. The fight was so quick, I was certain that he would have caught up to you. How did you escape?"

"I surrendered to the mark," Aramis answered.

Mel nodded. "I figured as much. As I lay dying, I heard singing. I thought I was imagining it. I wasn't." The sounds of pursuit echoed into the corridor. Mel quickened his pace. "Zevea, the Goddess of Light, welcomed me when I died. She told me of Edria's demise and asked for my allegiance. She promised to avenge Edria's death and to restore my life."

They stopped at the end of a long hallway. A wooden door blocked the way. Behind them, Aramis heard the howling of Jackalwere growing nearer. Mel motioned to the door. "I cannot follow you inside. There is something more powerful than the magic of mankind guarding this door. I will wait here for you."

Aramis stared at the door. He was tired and sore. Every move he made caused his muscles to scream at him. He guessed that the bones of Mordum were somewhere beyond that door. He feared he didn't have the strength to continue. His resolve was like steel, but his body threatened to rebel against him. He was aware of Mel's eyes on him.

"Why did you decide to come back?" he asked. "You were free of this life."

"I was not free of responsibility."

"Responsibility to what?"

"To the world. To the people who were still here. If Mordum succeeds, everything will be gone. I could not continue through eternity knowing that."

Those words gave Aramis a boost of strength he didn't know he had. He summoned his blade. The familiarity of its hilt reassured him. He could do this. Nodding to Mel, he pushed the door open and stepped inside.

Darkness enveloped him. The ceiling did not glow like it did outside the room. The blackness felt tangible, like a thin layer of material that parted and swept around him. Aramis had the feeling that something was watching him. A chill crept through his armor and he shivered. The walls around him shuddered from an unseen force. As he continued forward, he held his left hand out in front of him so that he didn't run into anything.

Fire leapt into life directly ahead of him. A large brazier was the source of light. Behind it, the flickering flames illuminated a figure seated on a throne. He stepped forward slowly, his grip on the sword tightening. As he drew near, he gasped.

The figure on the throne was his father.

He knew that is was an illusion, but it seemed too real. His face was identical to the last time Aramis had seen him. The royal crown rested on his head in the exact place his father always wore it. He was sitting straight, but upon seeing Aramis, he leaned forward.

"My son, is that you?" he asked. Even his voice was the same. Aramis's heart fought against his mind, wanting to believe that his father was truly alive.

"You're not real," Aramis whispered.

"Am I not? Then how do you suppose I am here?"

"I ..." he did not have the answer.

"Tell me, my boy, why have you come here? Do you not know that this place is a trap?"

"I know," Aramis said. "The wizard told me what this place is."

"And yet you came anyway?"

"Yes."

His father nodded slowly. "You were always brave. Nothing like your brother."

"My brother?"

The older man sighed and Aramis realized how aged his father looked. "There are many things I wanted to tell you. Some of them, such as this, I kept from you for your protection. I was going to reveal it to you before I died. At least, I intended to. Come closer." His father beckoned him.

Still unsure, Aramis kept his guard up, ready to strike. He inched closer. His father waited patiently as he took his time.

"I will not harm, my son. That is not why I am here. But *they* will." He nodded toward the darkness. Aramis looked to the edges of the firelight and saw shadowy figures moving about.

"What are they?" Aramis asked.

"Twisted creatures. Servants of the god of the dead. Never mind them," he said. "There is something you must know. Your brother is a vile man. The atrocities he committed are the reason I banished him from the kingdom."

"What did he do?"

"Many terrible things, all of them done in fear. I told him that he would not inherit the throne if he did not stop his dallying with the common people of our realm. He had many illegitimate children. He had them all killed, even those who had yet to be born." Tears trailed down the old man's face.

"Your mother was heartbroken, both at his actions and my decision. She was pregnant with you when it all came to light. Your brother had been angry. He's angry still, and he will not rest until he finds you."

"He won't have to," Aramis said. "I will take back the throne. By force, if necessary."

"It will not be an easy task," his father said. "Adamar is clever as a serpent and he has found favor with Mordum. You will need strong allies to fight the coming battle."

"I'm afraid," Aramis said.

"I know, my son, but you must persevere. If you fail, Mordum's darkness will sweep over the world."

"Is there no one else who can bear this burden?"

"Possibly," his father replied. "I am not gifted with visions of the future. Mordum has his gaze set on you, though I do not know why. My time here draws to its end. There is one more thing I must tell you. There are three things Mordum seeks. His blood, his bones, and his ashes. His blood you know of, his bones are here in this room, and his ashes are hidden beneath the castle."

"What castle?"

"Your castle. In the dungeon, there is a secret network of tunnels. Melchiades knows the entrance. The ashes are buried there. If your brother hasn't found them yet, he soon will. You must stop him from completing the ritual that will allow Mordum to take human flesh." The image of his father began to dissipate.

"Father, I don't know if I can do this. It's too big!"

His father smiled, and then he was gone. Before the flames in the brazier went out, he saw two things. The bones of Mordum sitting on the throne, and the shadows alive with movement. Aramis sprinted to the throne.

● ∞ ● ∞ ●

"My Lord," Mel interrupted. "We must be going if we plan to make it to the ship."

Aramis checked the hourglass at the bar and knew Mel was right. They could still make it if they hurried. "I'm sorry, but I must be on my way. Thank you for the food."

"Wait," Jarrod pleaded. "What happened? Did you get the bones?"

Aramis glanced to Mel who shook his head. Not seeing any danger in telling the boy, Aramis smiled. "I did. After fighting off the creatures that waited in the shadows, I escaped the room. Mel and I made it out of the Nexus to find that one of Mordum's armies was attacking the wizard's domain. My friend Kedrick was killed, but with the aid of the wizard, we were able to get away." A look from Mel cut Aramis's retelling short. "I'm sorry, but we must be going now."

"Thank you," Jarrod said. "I wish you luck on your journey."

"I appreciate it. We'll need everything we can get."

After Aramis and Mel left, Jarrod cleared the table and went to the back of the inn. He washed the dishes and helped his father start the fire in the kitchen's stove. Once the workers arrived and he was satisfied his father had ample help, Jarrod left the inn. He walked a few streets northward and turned down an alley. Glancing around to make sure he wasn't followed, he knocked on the backdoor of one of the dilapidated buildings.

The door partially opened and a robed figure peered out at him. "Is it done?" the man asked.

"It's done," Jarrod answered. "I put the poison in their food. He and his priest friend ate all of it."

"Well done," the man said.

"One more thing. He told me they have the bones."

"You have more than earned your reward." The man opened the door fully. Jarrod stepped inside and the man closed the door behind him.

"Prepare yourself to receive the Mark."

—Melchiades

CHAPTER 8

Shortly after leaving port, Aramis became ill. It began as a minor stomachache, but quickly progressed. He gripped the worn wooden frame of his bed and vomited into a bucket. Mel hovered around him like a distraught mother, but there was nothing he could do.

"Perhaps," Aramis choked, "I ate something that didn't agree with me."

Mel shrugged helplessly. "I don't know, my Lord."

Aramis laid back on his bed. His lips were chapped and felt like they were burning with fire, while his mouth was dry and tasted of the vile acids of his stomach. He was light headed from the heaving. His vision swam before him and he thought for a moment that he might pass out. He held onto consciousness, however, and looked to his friend. Mel had a worried look on his face.

"I need some fresh air," Aramis croaked.

"The windows don't open," Mel answered. "I've

already tried them. I can carry you out on deck, if you feel up to it?"

Aramis debated with himself for long moments before nodding his head. Mel helped him out of the bed. Aramis placed his arm around Mel's neck and the two staggered from their cabin to the open deck above.

The smell of saltwater and the sound of waves lapping against the hull greeted them. Aramis breathed in deep, trying in vain to make the stench of vomit leave his nostrils. They passed the Captain on their way to the railing.

"Put me down," Aramis said. Mel helped him to sit on the deck with his back to the rails. The Captain walked over to them.

"Gods man," he said. "You look like a demon from Hell."

"I feel like I'm in Hell," Aramis replied. The roof of his mouth felt like dried leather and the light headedness had been replaced with a splitting headache. He closed his eyes and enjoyed the mild afternoon breeze that blew across the deck.

"That's the worst case of seasickness I've ever seen," the Captain muttered to Mel.

"I don't think that is what he's suffering from," Mel replied softly.

"It's not the plague?" the Captain asked alarmingly. He took a step back.

"No, not at all. I've seen something like this before, years ago. It was poison."

"Poison?" the Captain said.

Mel nodded. "Deadly nightshade, if all of the symptoms hold true."

The Captain stared at Aramis in concern. "He needs help, and soon. I'd wager he'll be dead in a day, two at the most."

"Not if I can help it," Mel replied. The Captain

clapped Mel on the shoulder and then strode away.

"You know I can hear you," Aramis said. "The wind carries quite well down here."

"I know you can."

"If I die—"

"Don't," Mel interrupted. "You are not going to die."

Aramis sighed. The two remained silent.

"Did you hide the bag?" Aramis cracked his eyes at Mel.

"I did. It's under a loose floor board beneath your bed."

Aramis noticed one of the sailors nearby taking an interest in their conversation. He opened his eyes fully and stared at the man. The sailor met his gaze momentarily before turning away. Aramis was too tired and give it any thought.

"I think some sleep will help me," he said. Mel helped him to his feet and took him back below deck and placed him in his bed. Aramis knew Mel wouldn't leave his side, so he didn't bother telling him to go. He closed his eyes and darkness overtook him.

Dry, brittle grass crunched beneath his boots. A few feet away, he could see a fountain that showered water droplets into a small pool. He suddenly realized he was thirsty. He walked to the fountain and knelt beside it, reaching his cupped hands in. Scooping the water up, he drank some. It burned his mouth and his throat.

Instinctively, he spat it out and flung it from his hands. Before his eyes, the water turned colors. It became black and oily. A shadow moved beneath the surface of the water. Aramis stood up and back away warily.

The shadow slowly lifted from the water. It had the form of a man, yet it had no defined features. The shadow stepped out of the pool. Whatever it touched quickly turned black and oily like the water that had spawned it.

Aramis tried to summon his blade, but nothing happened. The shadow approached him. Aramis backed away, only to be stopped by something tall and flat. He risked a glance. It was a wall. It stretched the length of his vision. He turned back to the shadow.

Its arm reached out toward him. Dark, oily water dripped from its fingers. It grabbed him and he screamed in agony. A searing pain shot through his body. He gasped and tried to push the shadow's hand away, but his hand slipped through the shadow. He couldn't touch it!

The shadow's other hand gripped his throat and began to squeeze. He choked and struggled, but the shadow did not relent. And then he died. He knew the feeling. It was familiar to him. Although he was dead, he was still aware. The shadow dropped him to the ground.

Aramis felt the life come back into him. He pushed himself up and stood before the shadow. This time, it did not touch him. Hesitantly, Aramis reached out and touched the shadow. It immediately collapsed upon itself and splashed to the ground.

Aramis awoke to screams and smoke. He sat up and immediately noticed he no longer felt ill. He was, however, extremely weak. His cabin door was open and Mel was missing. Summoning his armor and sword, he staggered feebly out of the door and up onto the deck.

Chaos was everywhere. Sailors were battling each other. The clash of steel filled the air. Aramis quickly spotted Mel. He was back to back with the Captain and they were surrounded. Aramis summoned his blade and lurched toward them. The ship swayed erratically. A quick glance revealed that no one was manning the tiller.

A sailor intercepted him mid-deck and engaged him. Aramis lifted his sword to parry the man's attack, but he was exhausted and offered a sloppy defense. Had he not been protected by his armor, the sailor would likely have ended the fight quickly.

His muscles screamed in reproach as he struggled to keep the sailor's blade at bay. The ship swayed hard to port and Aramis slipped, falling to one knee. The sailor managed to keep his balance and struck Aramis in the chest with his blade. The sword clanged off his breastplate and Aramis focused all his strength on swinging his own sword in a horizontal arc. His blade cleaved through the sailor's first leg and halfway through the other.

The sailor screamed and dropped to the deck, blood gushing freely from both extremities. Aramis's vision blurred from the exertion. He tried to move his body with the swaying of the ship as he waited for his vision to clear. As soon as it did, he saw the Captain get struck down by one of the sailor's. From his vantage point, he couldn't tell if it was a mortal blow or not.

The sailor he'd maimed continued screaming, rolling around the deck, washing the boards with his blood. Aramis rose to his feet and as he passed the fallen man, he drove his blade through the man's throat.

"Shut your mouth," he muttered to himself. He forced his burning muscles to obey him and made it to Mel's side.

"What are you doing?" Mel shouted as he struck a sailor in the nose with the hilt of his blade. His armor glittered brilliantly in the sunlight.

"I'm helping," Aramis answered. He attempted to block a blow from another sailor, but the force of the sailor's swing knocked Aramis's blade from his grasp. Mel whipped his blade around and stabbed Aramis's assailant in the stomach. The sailor collapsed backward, falling to the deck and holding his wound.

"You are too weak to be of help, my Lord," Mel said.

"What's going on?"

"Assassins," Mel answered. "Agents of Mordum."

"What are they doing here?"

"I have my suspicions, but I'm not sure. I think they are looking for the bones."

Aramis nodded. He suspected as much. "I can't tell friend from foe," he complained.

"Just kill anyone that attacks you," Mel said. "Can you check on the Captain?"

Aramis looked to where the man had fallen. A puddle of blood had pooled around him. Aramis knelt beside him and examined his wound. He'd been gashed across his chest. It wasn't mortal, but it was deep. Aramis retrieved his sword and cut the Captain's shirt off. Using the material like bandages, he covered the wound and tied it tightly around the man's chest. He groaned as Aramis worked. *That's a good sign,* he thought.

He slumped to the deck beside the Captain, holding his sword across his lap. He couldn't put up much of a fight in his state, but he was determined to defend the Captain from further harm. Within a few minutes, Mel and the few remaining loyal sailors had taken back control of the ship. Mel made his way back over to him.

"How's the Captain?"

"He's not in immediate danger, but he may get an infection. Does anyone know how far we are from the closest harbor?"

Mel consulted with one of the sailors and returned. "Two days sailing with a strong wind and a full crew. There aren't many of them left, though."

"Unless there's a healer on board, the Captain won't make it two days."

One of the sailors began shouting and pointing. Mel looked and shook his head.

"What is it?" Aramis asked.

"We've got a bigger problem," Mel answered. "We're close to show and we're about to run aground."

A splintering crash shook the entire ship and sent everyone sprawling. Although Aramis was already sitting, he fell flat and went sliding across the deck, slamming hard into the main mast. The wounded captain slid across the deck and would have fallen into the sea if it weren't for Mel. He managed to grab the captain's boot and hung on with all the strength he had as they tumbled along the deck.

The ship immediately listed and tilted starboard. The remaining sailors scrambled madly, dashing in different directions. A few moments later, as Aramis struggled to his feet, one of the sailors appeared from below deck.

"She's taking on water!" he yelled. "Abandon ship!"

Gods, Aramis groaned, *could things get any worse?*

He staggered weakly toward Mel and the captain. Mel started toward him with a worried look on his face. "No," Aramis shook his head. "Help the captain. I'm all right. I just need some rest."

Mel hesitated but aided the captain anyway. Mel lifted the man easily. "I don't think I can tread the water with extra weight," he said. "We'll need to get him on one of the boats."

They headed to the side of the ship where the sailors had gathered. They were lowering a boat with a few men into the water with a system of pulleys. Once it was safely on the water, the men in the boat pushed away from the ship and began paddling toward the shore.

"Everyone in the boat," Mel said to the few sailors left aboard the ship. "I'll lower you down, but you need to take the captain."

The men climbed into the boat and helped pull the captain over the railing. They eased him down onto one of the benches. Mel motioned for Aramis to get into the boat.

"You can't lower it yourself," Aramis said. "I'll help you."

"You can barely stand, my Lord. I don't think you'll be much help."

Aramis would have argued, but he was too exhausted to think. He nodded and climbed into the boat. Mel lowered the boat easily enough until the last four feet, when he lost his grip on the ropes. The boat dropped with a sudden jerk, slamming into the water. The captain groaned. The sailors waited to move the boat until Mel had leapt off the ship and into the water. He swam near and they pulled him into the boat.

As they paddled away, the timbers of the ship creaked and groaned like some kind of large animal that was slowly dying. Close to half an hour later, they reached the shore. Aramis waited to depart until the sailors had moved the captain out of the boat, mostly because he didn't know if he had the strength to.

He waved away offers of help and stepped out of the boat. He had the distinct feeling of falling before he saw the ground rushing up to meet him.

● ∞ ● ∞ ●

Aramis awoke feeling warmth against his skin. He turned his head toward the source and saw a small fire burning. The smell of something cooking made his mouth water. He grunted as he sat up and looked around. Mel was tending the fire and cooking. A few of the sailors sat around the fire, staring blankly into eternity. The captain lay a few feet away, his breathing shallow and uneven.

"We've got to help him," he said, but his words came out as nothing more than a croak. Mel looked at him and frowned.

"I'm afraid there's nothing we can do," he said softly. "If I could heal him, you know I would."

Aramis watched the wounded man in silence. *I can't*

82

stand to see anyone die, he thought. *How am I going to kill my own brother if it comes to that?*

His thoughts were interrupted when Mel handed him a piece of wood with some sort of pinkish meat on it.

"Fish," Mel said, as if reading his mind.

"Thanks." Aramis ate in silence, watching the captain the entire time. The sun was quickly descending and the temperature was beginning to drop. "How long was I out?" he asked.

"A few hours," Mel answered.

Aramis sighed. He didn't know exactly where they were, but he knew they were still a long way from Oakhaven. It would take them weeks to reach on foot, even longer once they got closer to the castle. His brother was sure to have troops patrolling the entire kingdom. He glared at the fire, cursing the gods for ruining his life. Everything had been perfect. He had no need to worry about being king for many years because his father had been in perfect health.

But now ... everything had changed. Even if he took the throne back from his brother, life would never be the same. It could never be the same. He looked over to see Mel staring at him.

"Are you well?" Mel asked.

Aramis nodded. "Physically, I'm fine. Mentally? I've got a lot on my mind."

The sailors finished their meals and worked to pull the boats further up the beach, intending to use them for beds. After they had settled down for the night, only Aramis, the captain and Mel remained by the fire.

"I don't know if I can do this," Aramis said suddenly.

"What do you mean?"

"All of this." Aramis waved his hand. "I don't know if I can do what I need to. What if my brother refuses to give me the throne? What if I must take it by force? Many innocent people will die for something that won't affect them."

"Tell me, my Lord, how does this not affect the people? The one who sits upon the throne has more to do with the commoner's lives than you may realize. He dictates the taxes, appoints the nobles, commands the generals and the armies. If the wrong man rules the land, do you not think that his decisions, good or ill, will affect the people?"

Aramis knew Mel was right. He had learned a lot from his father about being a king, even though he never thought he'd have to worry about kingly responsibilities for several years. "How can I kill my brother?"

"How could your brother have your father assassinated?"

"That's different," Aramis said.

"Exactly my point," Mel countered. "What your brother did was evil. What you will do, if you do it, will be justice."

"It's not about justice." Aramis paused. "It's about the reckoning," he whispered. "I want him to pay for *everything* he's done. I want to kill him, but I fear that if I take that path, I may never come back from it."

Neither spoke for long moments. "What are the sailors going to do? Are they coming with us?" Aramis changed the subject.

"No," Mel shook his head. "I spoke to them while you were unconscious. They're going to head back up the coast and try to find work on a new ship."

"What about the captain? What do we do with him? We can't travel far with him in his condition."

"I think the sailors will take him when they go."

Aramis rubbed the stubble on his chin. "It's my fault."

"My Lord?"

"The shipwreck. It's my fault. Mordum's agents are after me. If that were not the case, these people would be alive and sailing."

"Possibly," Mel said. "All men die at some point."

"They shouldn't have had to die early." Aramis lay down and stared up at the sky. "I'm going to sleep."

"Good idea, my Lord."

At some point, his eyes got heavy and he drifted off to sleep. He awoke the next morning when the sun was shining on his face. Groggy and sore, he sat up. Mel was still asleep, but the sailors were nowhere to be found. And they had left their captain behind.

"Blast them," Aramis muttered as he rose to his feet. He grabbed a water canteen that lay by the fire and drank deeply. The cool liquid soothed his parched throat. He relieved himself near the lapping waves and came back to check on the captain.

He was dead.

From what he could tell, the captain had been dead for a few hours. His skin was pale and his limbs had stiffened. Aramis kicked at the sand in anger. A noise startled him and he turned to see a familiar old woman. Her eyes were covered by a stained cloth and she was pushing a wooden cart that creaked as she walked.

"How …?" Aramis was at a loss for words. He hadn't seen her in a long while.

"How what, boy? How am I here?" she stopped pushing the cart and laughed. "I've told you before," she said. "Revelation—"

"Will come in time," Aramis finished for her.

"Took you long enough," the old woman cackled.

Aramis shook his head. "You say that it will come in time, yet I have more questions now than when we first met."

"Such is life for mortals. Come here, my boy. I will give you some knowledge."

Aramis stepped closer to her and she rested one hand on his shoulder and one on the side of his head. Aramis's vision swam and then he was looking upon a vast black ocean, only it didn't ripple like normal water. As he struggled to understand what he was seeing, tiny pinpricks of light began to sparkle across the black surface.

Suddenly, he felt very small. The black ocean wasn't an ocean at all, but the dark vastness of the sky and the tiny lights were a multitude of stars. Aramis staggered back, breaking free of the old woman's touch.

"What … what did I see?" he asked.

"An impression. I can only show you a glimpse, lest you fall into madness."

"I don't understand."

The old woman cackled gleefully. "Your mind is a fragile thing! It can only accept so much. To show it more would drive you to insanity."

"It was like …" Aramis struggled for words. "Like seeing the sky and the stars, but not from here. From above, looking down."

The old woman smiled and nodded. "Exactly."

"Holy Goddess!"

Aramis turned to see Mel staring in wonder. His friend took a few steps, then knelt before the old woman. In that moment, Aramis realized something he had overlooked, though he couldn't recall noticing it before. When Mel had first found him in the Nexus, his armor had a new symbol—a sun with outstretched wings, the mark of Zevea. The old woman's cart had the same symbol etched into the wood on the sides. As though scales had been removed from his eyes, Aramis suddenly had an epiphany.

"You're … a goddess, aren't you? You are Zevea?"

"In the flesh," the goddess answered.

"I'm confused. I thought the gods were immortal beings that lived … up there?" Aramis motioned to the sky.

"We did, but now we walk among you in flesh and blood. We live as you live, but we too can die as you die." Her face turned sad.

"How?"

"It is not easily explained, but I will try. Long ago, before the stars were born, there were five of us. Alandren, the god of strength. Edria—" the goddess paused at the name, "the goddess of knowledge. Tael, the god of valor, whom you have met before. Mordum, the god of the dead. And myself, the goddess of light. We five created this world and the races that live upon it. We sought to create a balance in the expanse. There was only darkness before creation. I created the sun, the moon, and the stars. Alandren created the world, Edria created the races, Tael gave them strength to survive, and Mordum set the limit of their lifespan.

"As the people flourished, we five made an agreement. We would bless those who devotedly sought us, giving them armor and weapons. In return, their faith strengthened us. We also agreed never to directly interfere with the events of this world. But one of us did not keep this arrangement."

"Mordum," Aramis said knowingly.

Zevea nodded. "Yes. He broke the agreement and came to the world as a mortal, but with all his godhood. He tried to gain more power for himself. He thought that if the people saw him in the flesh, they would know he existed and would believe in him, their faith increasing his power."

"But faith is believing in what you cannot see."

"You are correct, but Mordum did not want to see reason. He was full of greed and malice. As he killed and rampaged across the lands, his power grew because of the souls he was taking. Thankfully, with our guidance, mankind was able to stop him."

"Or did they? It seems like he's causing a lot of chaos

in the world right now."

"That he is," Zevea said. "When he was defeated the first time, we allowed a part of ourselves to empower the tools needed to stop him. What we did not know at the time was that in doing so, we lost our immortality."

Aramis considered some of the other religions that he had heard of, gods and goddesses not named by Zevea. "What of the other gods that people put their faith in?"

"We five were the originators of creation," the goddess answered, "but other minor gods came to our world. Though they were gods, they were not as powerful as us, and so we did not fear anything they might do within the world. That may have been one of our mistakes. The god who came to the world and called himself the Lord Aio inspired Mordum's betrayal."

"The man who battled Orlek?"

"The same."

Aramis digested her words. He had difficulty believing them. He'd never been a man of faith. He believed only in what he could see. During his journey, however, he'd found that there were many things that he could not explain.

"One of the other gods you mentioned. Tael. You said I've met him before?"

"Indeed. When the Prophet of Edria imprisoned you, he was there as well. He spoke to you."

The memory came back to him and he laughed at the absurdity of it. "A god was stuck in a prison?"

"Of course not," Zevea scoffed. "He could have left at any time. He stayed because he wanted to discern your character."

"Why?" Aramis asked.

"There is much more at stake than you reclaiming your throne. The gods are at war. Mordum has killed Edria, and he seeks the remaining three of us that still live. This is not a battle for a throne, Aramis. This is a battle for mankind. If he kills us, there will be nothing and no one who can stand in his way. Tael wanted to know if we could trust you, if you had the strength to deny the dark power that Mordum offers his followers."

"Did I pass his test?" Aramis asked brusquely. "I'm glad to know that the people's decisions don't matter, that our lives are just some pawns on a board that you gods play with." Aramis turned away from her, angry. Mel still knelt before her. That made Aramis even more angry. "What are you bowing for?" he demanded. "She's mortal, just like you and I. There's no reason to be worshipping her."

"She saved my life," Mel replied quietly. "That templar killed me. I was dying on the road and she saved me. She gave me my life back. That may not be worthy of anything in your mind, my Lord, but it is in mine."

His sudden guilt outweighed his anger. He shook his head in frustration. "I'm sorry. You know what I meant."

Mel said nothing.

Aramis turned back to Zevea. "What do we do, then? How do we defeat Mordum?"

"You will need the items that his followers have been collecting. The blood, the bones, and the ashes."

"Ashes?"

"Yes. They are the ashes of Mordum's body when he walked the world previously. When these items are mixed and the body of one of his servants is offered freely, Mordum will take over control of the body, destroying the soul of his follower."

"Where do we find them?"

"Your brother has already found them. They were hidden beneath the castle at Oakhaven."

"Great. We only have the bones."

"You have the blood *and* the bones," Zevea said.

"No," Aramis argued. "The traitor prophet has the blood."

"Edria's prophet is not a traitor. He was protecting you."

"By throwing me into prison? I must be missing something."

"You were bent on revenge for the death of your father. You were not strong enough to face Mordum's templar. You still aren't. He was protecting you from yourself."

"I don't believe it," Aramis growled. "Either way, I'm going to get the blood from him, even if I have to kill him."

"I don't think that will be necessary," Zevea kept her sightless gaze on him. "With Edria dead, his power is no more. He used the last of it to launch an attack against your brother and his guards. His armor and his blade are gone."

"I can't imagine the feeling," Mel said. He was standing now, shaking his head.

"So he has to find new weapons," Aramis said dismissively.

"When you've had the blessing as long as I have, you will understand. When you have the armor and blade, you can feel the closeness of the gods. If that presence was gone," Mel stared off into the distance. "You'd feel different. It would be like a piece of you were missing."

Aramis wondered if he'd feel that way once the mark of Mordum was no longer a curse upon his body. He imagined he would feel free again, but as he considered it more, he wondered if it would be worse not feeling the power. *Gods,* he thought, *I'm actually thinking of keeping the power. I've got to deny the temptation.*

"I will do what I can to stop Mordum," Aramis said, making his final decision. "But know that I do not do it for the sake of the gods. I do it for the people who suffer with you meddling in their lives."

If his words bothered her, she did well to hide it.

"Good. I have something that will help you on your way. It will speed your journey." Zevea opened the top of her cart and reached inside. She dug around for a moment before pulling out two small objects. She handed one to each of them.

Aramis held up and inspected it. It was a wooden figurine of a horse. It was intricately carved, with all the details of a real horse. "What am I supposed to do with this?" he asked.

"You will summon the spirit of the animal that is bound to it. Put it on the ground and speak the word *'Capall'*. The spirit will come to you and take you wherever you need to go."

"'Capall," Aramis repeated. Suddenly he felt a strong vibration in his hand. The wooden figurine trembled in his hand. He tossed it to the ground on instinct, which saved him from injury. As it fell through the air, the figure of a large horse materialized. The figurine landed in the sand next to the horse. Aramis stared in awe and surprise. The horse was identical to the figurine.

"Next time, make sure you place it on the ground first. I'd hate to see you get crushed by a few hundred pounds."

Mel placed his on the ground and repeated the word. Within moments, another horse had materialized.

"They can travel longer than a horse of flesh, but they still must rest. They are spirits, so they will need to return to their realm. To dismiss them, you must say *'dhíbhe'*. If you run them too long, they will dissipate on their own, whether you are still mounted or not."

"Thank you, Holy Goddess," Mel said with a bow. "We appreciate these gifts."

"Will you be there when you are needed?" Aramis asked Zevea. "When we confront my brother?"

"I will be near," she answered. "You will need all the help you can get if you hope to stop Mordum."

Aramis turned to Mel. "Let's be off then. Maybe we can find a town to eat at. I don't really care to eat more fish."

Mel chuckled. "I agree, my Lord."

"Until we meet again," Zevea said. Then she continued pushing her cart along the beach.

Aramis mounted the spirit horse and pressed his lower legs tightly against the horse. He urged the horse forward, holding onto its mane with his hands. He let the horse walk until he felt secure, then urged the horse to speed up. He looked over his shoulder and saw that Mel was not far behind.

If the gods thought to use him like a tool, they had a rude awakening coming. He refused to be pawn in their game.

They rode for nearly an hour in silence before they saw signs of life. Several people walked along the road ahead of them, headed in their direction.

"We should keep our guard up," Mel suggested. "I know we are far from Oakhaven, but I would not underestimate the reach of Mordum's servants." Aramis nodded wordlessly in agreement.

As they neared the group, it became evident there was nothing to worry about. The people were dirty and appeared to be carrying everything they owned. They moved to the side to allow the horses by. Aramis stared at them as he passed, wondering how they had come to look so pitiful. They continued following the road and eventually left the people behind, only to encounter another group in a similar condition.

Eventually, the road was crowded with people. Most of them looked like farmers or traders and almost none of them spoke. The air about them radiated hopelessness. Some of the people led livestock while others carried or herded small children.

"I wonder where these people are coming from," Aramis said with a glance to Mel.

"Hail," Mel called out to one of the farmers. "Where are you going? And where do you come from?"

The haggard man walked next to a woman whom Aramis assumed was his wife. Two younger girls, likely his daughters, stayed close by his side.

"We're going anywhere that will take us," he answered. "And we've come from Ravencliffe."

"Why are all these people on the road with you?" Aramis asked.

"Haven't you heard? The town has been raided and burned." The man's wife choked up and started to sob quietly.

"By who?" Aramis asked.

"The king."

Aramis stopped his horse. "What are you talking about?" The man backed away warily. "I'm not going to hurt you," Aramis said. "What do you mean the king raided the town?"

The farmer ran his dirty hand through his even dirtier hair. "I don't know how you haven't heard," he said. "The king has been terrorizing everyone. He's looking for the prince that murdered his father. When his soldiers were told that no one knew where he was, they destroyed everything." The farmer placed his arm around his wife comfortingly. "We've lost everything we've known. So, we're leaving to find a new place to start over. But I'm afraid that no matter how far we go, those soldiers will just continue to follow us."

"I'm sorry to hear of your troubles," Aramis said. A deep hatred was boiling up within him. How could his brother do such terrible things to the people that he was supposed to serve? He reached into a pouch on his belt and pulled out a few coins. "It's not much, but please, take it."

The farmer stared at him. "Who are you?" he asked.

"Someone who cares," Aramis answered.

"You might need it," the farmer said. "The soldiers have set a blockade outside of the town. They are charging for passage, in or out."

"Take it," Aramis insisted. "I'll be fine."

The farmer hesitated for a moment, then accepted the money. "The gods bless you!" he called out as Aramis nudged his horse onward.

"The gods can go to Hell," Aramis muttered under his breath. Once they got clear of the people on the road, Aramis spurred his horse and thundered down the road. Mel followed suite. He could tell from Aramis's demeanor that he was beyond enraged. *Zevea help anyone that gets in his way*, Mel thought.

—Melchiades

CHAPTER 9

It was nearing noon when they reached the rolling hills that marked Ravencliffe's borders. Aramis reined in his horse, jerking on the bit so hard that the animal grunted. Ahead, the smoke of the burning town hung in a thick haze and some of the buildings were still aflame. Aramis watched the thatched roof of one of the buildings give way in a shower of sparks. A few feet away, a copse of oddly swaying branches caught his attention. As the smoke swirled, the truth became clear. The trees were gibbets, and a dozen bodies hung from their branches.

His anger burned as hot as the flames around him. He stood in his stirrups and surveyed the rest of the town. Spotting a large gathering of people, he nudged his horse in their direction. As he got nearer, he counted four guards. Two were standing idle, while the other two were harassing people trying to pass. A long line of people stretched down the road, all of them trying to flee somewhere safer. The guards were extorting money, goods and even livestock as passage fees.

A few people were allowed to pass through the blockade at the cost of all the money they had on them. The guard stopped a woman with two small children.

"Please," she begged. "I don't have anything to pay with. I've lost everything." Behind her, the ill-clad children clutched at her and huddled together.

"I don't believe you, wench! Now pay the fee."

"That or you can trade one of the children," the other guard said. "I like children," he added with a leer. He reached toward one of them and the woman screamed.

"Get away from them," Aramis said. He summoned his blade and the air hissed as it formed. The crowd gasped and backed away from the blockade.

The guard who had reached for the child turned to face him. "Well, well. A rogue on a horse. Likely stolen, too. Mind your business, fool."

"Get away from them," Aramis repeated. He heard the air hiss behind him as Mel summoned his own blade. He moved his horse forward until he was between the guards and the helpless woman.

The guard drew his sword. "This is none of your business." The other guard drew his blade as well, but the two standing idle only had their hands on their pommels.

"I've just made it my business," Aramis said. "I suggest you and your fellows remove this blockade and get back to the castle."

"What are you going to do?" The guard sneered at him. "You're outnumbered."

"Is that so?" Aramis asked as he summoned his armor. The black metal formed around him and it felt different this time, stronger, more powerful. The guard exchanged uncertain glances with his fellow and then swallowed hard.

"You'll have to kill us all," he said. The other two guards unsheathed their swords and advanced toward him.

"With pleasure," Aramis said. His ebony blade glinted in the sun as he brought it down hard. The child-loving guard brought his own sword up to block, but it shattered under the force of Aramis's blow. Aramis wheeled his horse around, knocking the backside of the animal into the man. He staggered backwards and landed on the ground. As the horse came about, Aramis leveled his blade and swung horizontally, catching the other guard at the neck, just under his helm. The blade cleaved through bone and sinew. The guard's head dropped to the ground, followed quickly by his body. The other two guards slowed their advance, approaching cautiously.

Strike them, a voice bade him. *Strike them down.*

His heart was drumming in his head, pounding loudly in his ears. His hand clenched tightly around the handle of his sword. He swung out of the saddle, landing on the ground with a heavy thud. The guards, thinking they had the advantage, rushed him. He cut them down with little effort. He'd experienced the blood rage of battle before, when adrenaline coursed through his veins. Yet this feeling was something different, something darker.

He turned his attention to first guard who was still on the ground, not quite recovered from the horse hit. Aramis stalked toward him.

"Please," the man said, "I'm sorry. I was only following orders!"

Aramis barely heard the words. He closed the distance and placed the tip of his blade to the man's neck. "Beg for mercy," Aramis said.

The guard was terrified. A puddle formed under the man as he urinated on himself.

"Mercy!" he cried out. "Please, give me mercy!"

The tattoo on his arm began to pulse. Aramis could hear voices whispering, but he couldn't make out the words. Images flashed through his mind in a whirlwind. Death and destruction, visions of Mordum and his servants plunging the world into darkness, Oakhaven burning. The one that finally broke him was Hannah. Her body lay strewn on a roadside, naked and battered. A man he didn't recognize laughed as he tossed a coin onto her dead body.

Then the images were gone. Aramis shook his head, trying to clear the things he had seen from his mind. The guard stared up at him, trembling in fear. "Please," he whispered. "Mercy."

Aramis drove his blade through the man's throat. He made a choking sound as blood poured from the wound and out of his nose and mouth.

"Death," Aramis vaguely heard himself say, "is mercy."

● ∞ ● ∞ ●

"You didn't have to kill him," Mel said quietly. Sunset had come and they sat around a small fire. They had dismissed their spirit horses for the night and made camp outside the town of Ravencliffe. Most of the refugees had continued on, but a few had stayed. They had thanked him countless times, especially the woman he had rescued. The people had also offered him gifts, the only things they had with them. He'd gently refused, knowing they needed more help than he did.

"Yes, I did."

He picked up a stick and poked at the coals, then threw a few small branches into the fire. "He would have done it again to someone else."

"How do you know that?" Mel asked. "You could have scared him enough to make him leave that life behind."

"Doubtful," Aramis replied. "Those inclinations are bound deep in the heart. It would have taken the power of a god to change him. And the only god he seemed want to follow was Mordum."

"So, you are judge and executioner? Can you see into the hearts of men now?"

Aramis felt the tattoo on his arm burn. He looked at Mel. His friend stiffened. "What is it?" Aramis asked.

"Your eyes. They're worse."

Now that he mentioned it, Aramis noticed that his eyes did feel dry. "Must be the smoke," he said. "I think it's drying them out."

"No, they are getting darker. The blackness ... it's noticeable." Mel summoned his sword and offered it to him. Aramis took it and tilted the blade at an angle, using the firelight to see the reflection of his eyes. Peering back at him were two large black orbs. Aramis dropped the blade and stood up. His heart started pounding and he looked around in panic. *My eyes! What do I do?* His mind screamed.

Mel's voice cut through the fear. "My Lord, please sit down."

Aramis tried to calm himself. He sat back down and stared into the fire. *The power is changing me,* he thought. He could feel Mel staring at him. *What does he think of me now? What happens if this power takes control of me? Will Mel kill me?*

As much as he tried to convince himself that Mel would never try to, the thought nagged at him. "I'm going to sleep," Aramis said. He left the fire and laid a few feet away after taking his shirt off to use as a pillow. Not long after, he heard Mel put the fire out. Aramis stared up at the stars, his thoughts tormenting him worse than any physical pain could. His night was sleepless.

The next morning, despite being exhausted, Aramis's mood improved. He could feel the beginning of a headache, likely from not sleeping. His muscles ached and he didn't want to get up, but he knew that time was something they lacked. He sat up and looked for Mel. His friend was cooking breakfast. He put his shirt on and walked over to the small crowd that had formed around Mel. A couple of refugees were talking with him.

"It's worse the further you go," one of the men said. "The new king is a tyrant."

Some of the other nodded their ascent.

"Anyone who tries to fight back is punished. I've heard stories. Someone told me their brother was taken to the dungeons and tortured. They took a bucket of rats and placed it on his stomach, then put hot coals on the top of the bucket. Once it got hot enough, the rats tried to escape."

The man paused. "They burrowed through his flesh."

Mel remained silent, but Aramis saw the disgust in his friend's eyes.

"I go to stop him," Aramis said.

The people turned to see who spoke.

"Who are you?" the man who had been speaking asked.

"Aramis, prince of Oakvalor." There was a moment of silence before a few of the people began to kneel.

"Hold on," the man said. "You don't know this man from a beggar in the streets. How do we know he's really the prince? From what I hear, he murdered his father for the throne. He's the reason we're in this mess."

"I am the prince, but I did not kill my father." Aramis turned his arm to display the tattoo on it. "I was cursed by the god of the dead with this mark. The man who claims to be king is my brother, banished long ago for dark crimes. He's responsible for my father's death, not me."

The man eyed Aramis, his uncertainty evident.

"I will make him pay for everything he's done. I will restore everything he has destroyed. Your homes, your crops, everything."

"You can't bring back the dead," the man said, his tone softer.

"No, I can't," Aramis replied. "I lost my father to an assassin's blade. I know the sting of loss. I know too, the anger that burns beneath the grief. I will do everything in my power to right the wrongs he has committed. I swear it."

"I don't know if you are really the prince or not," the man said, "but I can hear the conviction in your words." He looked around at his fellow refugees. "I'll follow you."

The people in the crowd began to voice agreement, pledging their loyalty to him. "Please," he interrupted. "The path I walk is a dangerous one. I would never ask any of you to put yourself in peril."

"You didn't ask," the man said. "We volunteered. He may have killed your father, but my daughter was killed by his men on his orders. I will take up my sword and fight in her memory."

Aramis considered the man's words and knew he could no more deny the man's right to revenge than he could deny bread to the hungry. "If only I had a few thousand more men like yourself," Aramis said.

The man straightened with pride. "I don't know about that many, but if you are looking for men who want to fight against that tyrant, I know a few. I'll get word to them."

"Thank you," Aramis said. "Gather anyone you can find willing to fight, and meet me in ten days outside of Oakhaven."

After they ate breakfast and the refugees had departed, Aramis summoned his spirit horse.

"It's a few days' ride from Oakhaven," Mel said. "Why did you tell them to wait so long?"

"We're going to make a stop along the way," Aramis answered.

"Where at?"

Aramis mounted his horse and adjusted his position in the saddle until he was comfortable. "We're going to the Temple of Edria."

● ∞ ● ∞ ●

The scene that greeted them when they reached Kaldore two days later gave Aramis pause. At least a hundred refugees crowded the city. So many makeshift tents littered the streets, there was no room for wagons to pass by. Not that there were any wagons to speak. Trade, it seemed, had all but halted. Several priests roamed among the people, handing out meager portions of food and spare clothes and blankets.

Seeing the plight of his people added to the hatred for his brother that was already on the verge of boiling over. They pushed their way through the crowds and made their way toward the temple. Aramis felt a nervousness building within him as they got closer to the temple grounds. He remembered the betrayal of the Prophet. Although Mel had explained the Prophet's actions, he still felt the bitter sting of treachery when he thought of the man.

They only saw a few priests within the courtyard of the temple. Aramis assumed that most of them were out in the city, doing what they could to ease the troubles of the people. The large wooden doors were wide open, allowing free passage in or out. Mel took the lead and navigated through the various halls to an all too familiar door.

Aramis thought he saw the shadows flicker with life. Dark whispers filled the air around him. Distracted by them, he didn't notice that they had entered the Prophet's chamber until the man's voice echoed through the space.

"Melchiades?"

When he'd first met the man, he had been impressed. Now, Aramis barely recognized him. The Prophet's once muscular frame was now on the flabby side. His hair was disheveled and unkempt and his jaw had the faint beginnings of gray hair. The pendant he normally wore around his neck, a closed hand with an open eye in the center, lay on his desk.

"I thought you were dead," the Prophet said. He came around the desk and hugged Mel. "Had I known you were alive, I would have sent you help." As he broke the embrace, the Prophet seemed to notice Aramis for the first time.

"Ah, Prince Aramis. It does my heart good to know you are safe."

"No thanks to you," Aramis said. Mel shot him a look of disbelief, but Aramis ignored it. "I'm here for the blood."

The Prophet nodded. "I figured as much. Adamar has only sent one patrol here to try and claim it, but they did not find it so easy to overcome an old man." He chuckled. "I may not have my powers anymore, but I can still wield a blade."

"What news from Oakhaven?" Mel asked.

"Not much," the Prophet sighed. "The only visitors we get are refugees, and the only stories they have all sound the same. Death and destruction. You are free to anything you need, if we have it. There isn't much left. How did you survive the templar?"

Aramis felt his anger growing the longer he stared at the Prophet. He hated the man.

"I didn't. The templar mortally wounded me and I died, but Zevea brought me back."

"Zevea?" The Prophet's eyebrows rose in surprise. "Perhaps you can tell me the tale?"

"I'd love to, but perhaps another time. We still have a long journey ahead of us, and time is short."

"Of course," the Prophet waved his hands. "Please, follow me."

The Prophet led them through the temple to a room Aramis did not remember seeing previously. Withdrawing a key from the folds of his robe, he unlocked the door and directed them inside. The room was empty except for a small table in the corner of the room. Atop the table was a familiar item Aramis immediately recognized.

Blood. Blood. Blood. The dark voices began whispering the word repeatedly. It got faster, almost frantic. Aramis's heartbeat quickened in his chest as he got closer to the table. Aramis assumed it was his imagination, probably from his lack of sleep lately. Then his tattoo began to itch. He resisted the urge to scratch it. Mel reached for the wineskin that held the blood.

"No," Aramis said sharply. Mel and the Prophet exchanged glances.

"I'll take it." Aramis grabbed the wineskin from the table and strapped it to his belt. "We should get moving."

"Yes, my Lord."

"A word, if I may," the Prophet said.

Aramis shrugged. "Make it quick."

The Prophet looked to Mel. "I'd like to speak with him alone."

Mel frowned but nodded and left the room.

"The power is changing you, isn't it?" the Prophet asked.

"What do you know of power, priest? Your god is dead." Judging by the pained look on the man's face, Aramis knew he had struck a nerve. *Good,* he thought. *Let him suffer.*

"I know that Mordum uses the Mark to control his servants. For some, the power is too much. It brings madness. I can see the stain in your eyes, Aramis. The power is controlling you. Mel can see it, but I know he hasn't said anything. He doesn't want to confront you, but he must if you continue to get worse."

Aramis clenched his jaw. Deep down he knew the Prophet's words rang with truth, but something kept him from accepting it. A dark shadowy wall pushed the words from him.

"I may not have the gifts of my goddess anymore, but I can feel the darkness of Mordum radiating from you. You must fight the darkness!"

A torrent of hideous visions assailed Aramis. The dark whispers intensified and he staggered back, shaking his head. The Prophet stepped toward him, concern etched on his face. Suddenly, Aramis unsheathed the rusty dagger Zevea had given him and he plunged it into the Prophet's chest. The man's eyes widened in surprise. He opened his mouth as if to speak, but nothing came out.

Again, the voices whispered. *Again!*

Aramis jerked the dagger out and stabbed the Prophet again. The man fell to the floor, but Aramis's hatred was not satisfied. He knelt beside the Prophet and jabbed him with the blade over and over. When he finally stopped, he had no idea how long or how many times he had stabbed him.

His breathing was heavy and the muscles in his arms burned. Wiping the dagger clean on the man's clothes, he sheathed the blade. He considered hiding the body, but immediately discounted the thought. There was nowhere in the room to hide him, and Mel stood in the hall. *They'll blame it on the soldiers,* he told himself.

He looked himself over as best as he could to make sure there was no blood, then he left the room. Mel was leaning against the wall a few feet down the hall.

"Let's go," Aramis said.

"Where's the Prophet?" Mel asked.

"Praying," Aramis answered. "He said he wished he could go with us, but his duties here will not allow it."

Mel stared at him for a long moment. Aramis returned his gaze. "Come," Aramis bade and began walking. Mel fell into step beside him.

"Now that we have the blood, we must find the ashes," Aramis said. "The bones are still safe."

"How do you know?" Mel asked. "Didn't Vashah hide them with magic?"

"Yes," Aramis replied. "Vashah hid them, but I can feel their power. I know exactly where they are."

They left the temple and walked along the streets. Aramis knew time was something he severely lacked, but he wanted to make sure his people were being cared for. They spent the next hour talking with the refugees and helping the priests bandage wounds. Aramis listened to their terrible stories and would have wept with them, but no tears would come. Many of the people stared at him as if he were some sort of wild animal. He kept forgetting that his eyes had grown dark. After they saw his goodwill, their stares became less fearful.

"It's time," Aramis announced after they had finished putting together a few tents for a family of farmers. "It is time to go to Oakhaven. I want to do more for them, but I can't do that until I have reclaimed my father's throne."

"I fear we will not have enough men if it comes to war," Mel said later as they rode toward the capital. They saw less refugees the closer they got. Aramis had seen the road once before when it was bustling with traders coming in and going from Oakhaven. Now, it was desolate. Aramis wondered if anything would ever be the same.

Not if I die, he thought. He looked at Mel from the corner of his eye. The man had been his friend for years and had willingly given his life to protect him. Aramis considered his actions at the temple. He'd killed the Prophet, someone that Mel was close to. He searched his feelings, but he didn't find guilt. He did feel bad for Mel, knowing that at some point, he would learn of the man's death. It would be rough on him, but Aramis knew Mel was strong enough to get over the loss.

Something fell into his lap. Aramis looked down and saw that it was the pendant Hannah had given him. The chain had broken. Grabbing the chain before it fell, he wrapped the pieces around his belt. The beautiful woman's image came to his mind and he wondered where she was and if she were safe. He wondered, too, how her father had fared in drumming up support from the nobles for his cause.

"My Lord," Mel's voice shattered his thoughts. He looked to where Mel was pointing. A large contingent of soldiers was coming their way.

"Looks like we've lost the element of surprise," Aramis said as he summoned his armor and blade. The air hissed as Mel summoned his own. As the soldiers closed the distance, Aramis noticed they were all wearing the mark of Mordum as their insignia.

"I've got an idea," he said to Mel. "Dismiss your armor and your blade." After a moment of hesitation, Mel did as Aramis instructed. "Now hand me your reins."

Aramis pointed the tip of his blade at Mel. He slowed their horses to a stop as the soldiers hailed him.

"What's this?" one of them said as he pulled off his helm. He was clearly the leader, likely a captain. Aramis didn't recognize him. He had the typical short haircut of a soldier, but his face had distinct features that implied his noble birth. Aramis guessed he was the son of one of the nobles.

"I'm taking him to the king," Aramis answered. "Been searching for this dog for weeks, but I've finally caught him."

"Good work. I'll have some of the men escort him to the castle."

"That won't be necessary."

The captain leaned forward. "And why's that?"

"The king sent me specifically to track him down. If I wasn't the one to bring him back, I'd probably get the noose."

The captain eyed him suspiciously. "What's your name? And who do you report to?"

Aramis had no idea how the priesthood of Mordum was structured, but from everything else he had seen, it was similar to the other orders. He decided to bluff.

"That's not your place to ask, captain." Aramis dismissed his armor and displayed the Mark for him to see. The man's eyes immediately filled with fear.

"My apologies," the captain said quickly. "I didn't know you were one of them."

"Them?" Aramis asked.

The captain stammered. "Them, uh, one of the king's protectors."

Good to know, Aramis thought. "No harm done," he said.

The captain put his helm back on and bowed in his saddle. "We're looking for people who are trying to leave with the king's property. Have you seen anyone on the road?"

"Yes," Aramis lied. "A small group, about ten of them, were headed west toward Talvaard."

"Thank you," the captain said. He barked orders to his men and they rode off.

Once they were no longer visible, Aramis gave the reins back to Mel. "It seems my brother has Mordum knights as protectors."

"Why would a servant of Mordum need protection?" Mel said rhetorically.

"I think we'll find out soon enough."

They used the prisoner ruse twice more as they neared Oakhaven, but each time it was harder to pull off. Although the soldiers they encountered seemed fearful— reverent even—when he displayed the mark, they became more insistent about taking his "prisoner" themselves.

"The servants of Mordum, while they all seek to fulfill his purposes, have their own agendas. They will lie, cheat and kill anyone, including fellow servants, to gain Mordum's favor," Mel said after they left the most recent group of guards behind.

"Seems like chaos to me," Aramis remarked.

"When everyone is following the same delusion, with different intentions, chaos is sure to abound."

Aramis pondered Mel's words in silence as they continued south toward Oakhaven. It was nearing sunset and they still had several miles to cover, so Aramis decided they should stop soon and setup camp.

"If I may make a request," Mel said. "I'd like to stay at an inn."

"Do you think that's wise? We're close enough to be recognized by anyone working for Mordum."

"We could disguise ourselves," Mel suggested. "We're dirty and it's obvious to anyone that we've been on the road a while. Besides, I haven't gone this long without a bath in years."

Aramis shook his head, but he was smiling. "Ever the aristocrat," he chided jokingly. "Fine, but we need to keep out of sight as much as possible. If we get caught, everything we've worked for was in vain."

Mel's face went serious. "I won't allow us to be caught now, not after everything you've faced to get here."

They stopped for the night at a small village half a day's ride from Oakhaven. The sun had passed beyond the horizon and a breeze picked up. Aramis could smell rain coming. Dark clouds blotted out the moon and stars, making it hard to see more than a few feet ahead. Only a few lanterns had been lit and the wind made them sputter; their faint light flickering and causing the shadows to dance erratically.

Aramis eyed the dark shapes suspiciously. He felt like he was losing his mind lately. Seeing things in the shadows, hearing voices that weren't there ... but the grim visions were the worst. In the back of his mind, his thoughts always went to Hannah. Was the vision he saw real, or was it some evil joke sent from Mordum? He had promised himself that he would marry her. If she were dead ... he pushed the dismal thoughts away.

They found an inn down one of the side streets. No lanterns were lit, but the sound of music and boisterous conversation drew them in. The place was fairly full considering the current crisis that enveloped the kingdom. A fire burned in the hearth, tinging the air with the sharp smoky incense of too-green wood. Another smell, roasting pig, made Aramis's mouth water. Both scents were more pleasing than the others that wafted through the air: mercenary sweat and spilled food and drink that had been left for who knew how long.

"*Ugh*," Mel muttered beneath his breath. "It's too hot for a fire, especially with all these people. The heat is unbearable."

Aramis noticed that almost everyone looked like a mercenary. *No wonder the place is packed,* he thought. *They have no reason to be fleeing.* There was a small table in the corner available, so they sat there and waited for the barmaid. It took longer than Mel liked, and he huffed his indignance a few times, as though anyone other than Aramis could hear him. Finally, a young girl with sinuous sun-lightened hair that spilled down past her breasts came to serve them. She was wearing a flowing brown skirt that reached her knees and a cloudy white, almost transparent blouse that left little to the imagination. She leaned onto the table and made no attempt to hide the clear view of her cleavage through the V of her blouse.

"Drinks?" she asked with a grin.

Aramis didn't reply. He stared at her, his dark eyes catching her watery blue ones and holding them. Faint lines edged away from her eyes, though from exhaustion or worry, he didn't know. Her eyelashes were thick with kohl, the lids covered with a deep shade of purple. It reminded him of the nobles at court, who covered themselves with ridiculous shades of color, always trying to outdo one another. Finally, he looked away, and the woman blinked and shook her head as if to rouse herself from a dream. Her ample breasts swayed with the motion.

"I'll take a drink, and some food," Mel said. "We'll also need a room for the night," he added.

The woman looked at Mel as if just noticing him for the first time. "You're a handsome one, aren't you?" she said. Mel blushed, and she continued flirting with him. "Anything else you'd like? Anything you see that you might *want*?"

Mel looked away and caught Aramis's gaze. Aramis remained impassive to the exchange.

"You're both handsome," she said. "Your friend doesn't smile much, hm?" She made a soft huffing sound, angling her breath up with her lower lip, causing her collection of curls that hung over her forehead to flutter and resettle. She sauntered away and came back with a tray, her ample hips swinging. She placed two mugs of beer on the table and looked at Mel.

"Need company for the night?" she asked.

"I'd love some company," Mel replied, winking at her with one eye. "Unfortunately, I don't have much money."

The woman frowned with puckered lips. "Pity. I bet we could start a fire hotter than the one in this room." She flounced away to another table, flirting with the patrons there as well.

Aramis was scanning the room, looking for anyone that might appear to be a soldier of Oakvalor. The last thing they needed was to be recognized by someone. As he finished looking over the room for the second time, he noticed one man who stood out from the crowd. He definitely wasn't a mercenary, though he was too well dressed to be a refugee. He kept fidgeting, making Aramis think he was nervous. He decided it would be a good idea to keep an eye on him.

The barmaid returned with two plates of food and refilled their drinks. Aramis knew if he drank too much more, he'd begin to lose his focus. He continued to glance at the man occasionally.

"I think he's waiting for someone," Aramis said.

"What?" Mel replied through a mouthful of food.

"The man at the table there," he nodded with his head. "I think he's waiting for someone. We may want to watch him for a bit. There's something ... odd about him."

Mel finished his food and leaned close to Aramis. "Should I go talk with him? See if I can get anything out of him?"

Aramis studied the man closely. His clothes were from the Oakhaven court. At least, the current style that was in fashion before he'd left. He didn't have the bearing of a noble. A servant, perhaps?

The door to the inn opened and a man dressed in riding clothes entered. He swept the crowd with his gaze and then headed toward the fidgeting man. He sat down and the two began speaking. They were too far away for Aramis to hear their conversation.

"I'll be back," Mel said. He made his way toward the two men, but stopped within earshot and pretended to flirt with the barmaid. After a few minutes, Mel came back.

"I don't know who they are, but they know Lord Bavol," Mel said quietly. That perked Aramis's intrigue.

"Could you hear what they were talking about?" he asked.

"Somewhat. The lady certainly has a way with words. Anyway, the better dressed man is a servant to Bavol, I believe. From what I could make out, the rider delivered a letter to the king of Talvaard."

"Garrick?" Aramis asked. "I didn't realize he'd been coronated yet." He shook his head. "We're behind on current events. That could bode ill for our journey."

"Perhaps. The other man, the messenger, he said he had a return letter for Lord Bavol. He didn't say what it contained. He's concerned, though. Apparently, he was supposed to meet Bavol somewhere, but it didn't appear he was there, or had ever arrived."

Aramis felt his heart drop into his stomach. *The vision ...*

"Gods," Aramis sighed. "He was our key to the nobles. Without him, we don't know who is on our side." He rubbed his face.

"Maybe," Mel said, then paused. "Maybe we could speak to them. Figure out where they were supposed to meet. That might provide some clues as to where Bavol might be if he ran into trouble."

"They could be spies," Aramis said.

"That's true, though I don't believe so. They both seemed genuinely concerned for him."

Aramis steepled his fingers and stared at the two men in silence, biting on his lower lip. "I think it's worth the risk," he finally said. "The information Bavol has is pivotal to our next move. We don't have much time, though. We've only got a few days left."

"Until what?" Mel asked, confused.

Aramis smiled, the first time in a while. "While we were in Keswick, I sent a message to Lynessa."

"I vaguely remember that," Mel said, nodding.

"She promised me anything I needed if we helped her with the Warlock. I asked her to send her armies to Oakhaven."

Mel's surprise was sincere. "I had no idea!"

"I know," Aramis said. "I figured the less people who knew about it, the more of a surprise it would be to my brother when her troops showed up."

"Her armies alone should suffice if it comes to violence," Mel said excitedly. "Then there's the refugees who band together."

"And the druids," Aramis said. "I instructed Lynessa to send word to the druids as well."

"You didn't tell me about any druids."

"It was after … you were gone. Anyway, I helped them as well. They don't want war and they won't use their magic to harm anyone directly, but their help will be an invaluable defense against Mordum's dark magic."

"I must confess something," Mel said. "I will follow you anywhere, to any danger. You are my friend, my brother. But I had my doubts about whether or not we could do this. Now," Mel's eyes lit up, "now, I think we have a chance."

"That makes two of us," Aramis said.

"Talent is only the beginning. The real magic lies in perfection through relentless practice."

—Larson

CHAPTER 10

The messenger was the first of the two to leave. Shortly after, the other man followed. Bavol's men had stayed at the inn long enough for Aramis and Mel to take turns cleaning up while the other watched them to make sure they didn't leave.

They paid the barmaid and left the inn. The air had gotten cooler since their arrival, and it was a nice change to the stuffy inn. The servant didn't appear to be as nervous. He walked with a purposeful stride down the cobbled road, not paying any attention to his surroundings. *He's not concerned with safety,* Aramis noted.

The man walked for a quarter of an hour, still seeming oblivious to his pursuers. He kept turning down different side streets and even began to whistle a melody. Aramis was taking care to try and be aware of their surroundings, but his main focus was on the man they were following.

"My Lord," Mel whispered suddenly. "We're going in a circle."

Aramis looked around and realized they were passing the inn they had left earlier. The hair on his arms began to tingle as he realized the trap.

The man stopped walking and turned to face them. He continued his whistling a moment longer, then smiled mischievously.

"A couple of rogues, then? Seeking to cut my throat and take my purse?" He folded his arms across his chest. "You'll find more than you bargained for here."

Several men, armed and armored, stepped out of the shadows between the buildings.

"I think there's been a misunderstanding," Mel said, holding up his hands. "We just want to talk with you."

"Right," the man said. "I won't fall so easily to your highwayman tricks." He nodded at one of the men. He drew his sword and began to approach.

"I'm looking for Lord Bavol," Aramis said. "You're one of his men, aren't you?"

The man tilted his head in curiosity. "And you are?"

Aramis looked to Mel, then back to the man. "Aramis, rightful king of Oakvalor."

The man unfolded his arms and looked around. "You'd best be keeping that information quiet," he said. "Sheath your blade, Sergid. He's an ally. Let's go somewhere safer to talk."

He led them to one of the dark buildings a few spaces down from the inn. The man made sure no one was watching them, then led them inside. They paused in the doorway as he lit a lantern. The dim light illuminated what Aramis thought was someone's home.

"The people who lived here left a few weeks ago," the man said. "We've been using it for our network." He hung the lantern from a hook in the ceiling and motioned them in. The man he'd referred to as Sergid closed the door and took up a position in front of it.

"You can't be too careful these days. Especially with that despot Adamar on the throne."

Adamar, Aramis thought. *So, that's his name.*

"So I've heard," Aramis replied. "I've encountered a number of people on the road. Their stories are all similar. What's your name?"

The man bowed low. "I am Larson," he answered. "Humble servant to Lord Bavol and commander of his house guard."

"You fooled me back there," Aramis said. "Watching you at the inn, I assumed you were an anxious type."

"All part of the ruse," Larson grinned.

"How'd you know I was watching you?"

"Not all of those men were soldiers. At least, not ones loyal to Adamar. One of them caught your interest in me and gave me a hand signal. Pretending to be a bumbling servant was easy. I'm glad you weren't a rogue. We've had to kill too many of them." Larson frowned.

"I'm glad you aren't a spy," Aramis replied. "Do you really not know where Bavol is, or was that part of your ploy as well?"

"I wish it were," Larson answered. "He's been missing since he and Hannah left Oakhaven. They were supposed to go into hiding at a cabin he owns a few hours from here. According to the last missive he sent, Adamar had taken an interest in Hannah."

Aramis felt bile rise in his throat. He forced himself to swallow it. The gruesome images from his vision flooded his mind. Her mutilated body lying on the side of a road. A man he didn't recognize tossing a coin onto her body.

"Was there a specific road they would have taken?"

"We've checked every road out of Oakhaven," Larson said. "No sign of them. They would have taken a wagon, and we haven't seen any signs of passage near the cabin. It's almost as if they simply disappeared. We're all worried."

Aramis knew the feeling too well. "I think I might know where you can check, if you haven't already." He recalled the image of the road her body lay beside. There was a tall stone marker a few feet ahead, though it did not have any engravings or signs. "There's an old hunting path that branches off the main road heading north."

Larson shook his head and looked to Sergid. They both shrugged.

"It was one of my father's favorite places to hunt. All of the nobles know where it is."

"Can you draw a map of it?" Larson asked. "I'll have my men search it."

"I can do better than that," Mel chimed in. "I'll lead them there."

"I didn't get your name," Larson said to him.

"Melchiades, but most people just call me Mel."

"It's an honor," Larson said. "Is the path far from here?"

"A mile, maybe."

"Please, go with Sergid and show the men where this road is. If we can find them, I hope they are alive."

"A storm is coming in. Maybe we should hold off until morning?" Sergid asked.

Larson nodded. "True. I wouldn't want you getting lost in the night. Can you take them in the morning?"

Mel glanced at Aramis.

"We've got pressing business. I was hoping to reach Oakhaven tomorrow."

"How did you plan to enter the city?" Larson asked. "Adamar has it locked down tighter than a prison in Talvaard."

"That's where we needed Bavol. He was working to rally the nobles to our cause. I was hoping to get there without bloodshed. I was also hoping to take the throne back without war."

"Those are some high hopes, if I can be so bold. Adamar has the nobles by the balls, some by fear and others by loyalty. Some of them remember him when he was younger."

"Then what do we do?" Aramis asked.

"We can get you into the city," Larson said. "But what are your plans once inside? I don't think you can trust anyone, especially the nobles."

Aramis didn't know what he planned to do. He'd put all of his thought into getting there alive, he didn't think about what he'd do if he succeeded. "I'm ... not sure," he said. "I know that doesn't sound promising, but it's been Hell just trying to get here. Do you have any suggestions? You've obviously been in the city. Where should we stay? We've got to setup a place of operations. I've got an army headed this way."

"An army, you say? How large?"

"Lady Lynessa from Keswick is sending her troops to aide us."

Larson whistled. "That's great news. You're definitely going to need it. Adamar has those black robed priests that follow him around. They give me the chills. There's also been a lot of rumors that there's some sort of ceremony that's going to happen soon. We haven't been able to get the details, but it sounds like a big deal. Lots of mercenaries are showing up, too."

"Gods," Aramis growled. "This is getting more difficult to fathom by the minute."

"Sorry," Larson shrugged. "I'm just giving you the facts. Once we get you into the city, I think it would be a good idea for you to only travel at night, and only under guard."

"Won't having guards be conspicuous?" Aramis asked.

"Don't worry about that. No one will be any wiser. I'm sure you both are exhausted. There's beds upstairs. I suggest you get some rest. Tomorrow will come faster than you want it to."

"Thank you," Aramis said. "I appreciate everything."

"I'm just doing my duty to the crown," Larson said. "We'll keep the house guarded. Get some rest. Until tomorrow."

"Until tomorrow," Aramis said.

●　∞　●　∞　●

Aramis was plagued by nightmares. Each time he awoke—drenched in sweat with his heart rapidly pounding in his chest—he would convince himself to go back to sleep. And each dream was worse than the last. Every one of his senses were affected by the dreams, making them seem so real that he woke himself from crying out. After waking from the last nightmare, he realized that sunset was not long in arriving.

He used a hand mirror and a razor he had found in the room to shave his face. No matter how dirty and sweaty he got on the road, he hated the feeling of an unshaven face the most. After he finished, he stared at his reflection for a long while. He scrutinized every inch of skin. It had only been a few months since he'd fled his home, yet he seemed to have aged by many years. Bags under his eyes did little to help. And his dark eyes were like two black pits in his head. The sight unnerved him. He flung the mirror at the wall, shattering it. The floor was littered with shards of glass.

"My Lord?"

Aramis turned to see Mel in the doorway. He hadn't heard him come in. "Yes?"

"The men have prepared breakfast, if you are feeling hungry."

"I'll be down shortly," Aramis said.

"I'm going to show Sergid and a few others where the trail is. I'll be back as quickly as possible."

Aramis nodded. "I'll meet you in Oakhaven, then. Larson is taking me there today. We need to prepare for what's coming."

Aramis knew that Mel didn't like the idea of them traveling separate. The look on his face made that evident. But they both knew, too, that there was little choice in the matter. Lord Bavol had important information.

"Don't do anything rash," Mel said, only half-jokingly.

Aramis grunted in reply. After Mel left, Aramis went downstairs and ate a small meal. Although he was hungry, he just didn't feel like eating. Larson showed up shortly after and gave him a change of clothes. Aramis hadn't realized how dirty and torn his own were despite cleaning them the night before. The clothes were a drab shade of brown and made of cheap material.

"You'll stand out less," Larson explained. "We want as little attention on you as possible."

Aramis didn't argue. The sooner he was in the city, the better. He assumed they would have ridden horses, but Larson thought traveling on foot was a better idea.

"It's easier to hide without a horse," he said. "Patrols are everywhere."

It took a few hours to reach the city. They would have arrived earlier, but a large group of soldiers had caused them to take a roundabout approach to the city. Aramis assumed they would enter the city through the main gate with some sort of disguise. Instead, Larson led him to a sewer grate on the side of one of the walls. Larson glanced around, then lifted the grate up and motioned Aramis to get in the tunnel.

"Hurry," he said.

Aramis obeyed and climbed inside. The tunnel was small, only four feet high. He had to crawl on his hands and knees. He heard the gate close behind him.

"Where does this lead?" Aramis asked.

Larson laughed. "I don't think you want to know."

A few feet in and Aramis's hands touched something wet and slimy. A foul smell assaulted him. "Gods, please tell me we aren't in the sewer."

"We're not in the sewer."

"Then, where are we?"

"The sewer. I told you that you didn't want to know."

"Yeah," Aramis muttered.

Larson squeezed by him and guided their crawl. After a hundred feet, they reached a large open chamber lit with torches. Aramis was glad they didn't have light in the tunnel. There was no telling what he might have touched.

"I found this place shortly after Adamar took the throne. We haven't explored all the tunnels. Some of them are caved in. But this one leads out of the city. We use it to get in and out without being noticed. We'll wait here until nightfall, then we'll go up to the city."

"Up?" Aramis asked, looking toward the ceiling.

"Yes. This room is underground. There's a ladder against the far wall there," Larson pointed, "that leads into an alley between some shops."

"What do we do until then?"

Larson shrugged. "Make yourself comfortable?"

Aramis spotted a cot. "Is that clean?" he asked.

"Yes, I had one of my men bring it here earlier."

"Good." Aramis climbed into it and propped his arms behind his head. The minutes ticked by slowly. Larson pulled a dagger from his boot and began sharpening it with a whetstone.

Sssk, sssk, sssk. Pause. *Sssk, sssk, sssk.* Pause.

Aramis's eyes began to grow heavy. His long night of terrible dreams had finally caught up with him. He vaguely heard Larson continue to sharpen his blade. *Sssk, sssk ...*

His eyes opened and he felt someone touching his shoulder. He snapped his head up and reached for his attacker, only to realize it was only Larson.

"Sorry," Larson said. "I didn't mean to startle you. It's time."

"It's dark already?" Aramis asked, surprised. That was the first time he'd slept without having a nightmare.

"Yes. I was going to wait until I'd heard from Sergid, but no messenger has arrived yet. I'll take you up. There's a tavern you can use at night. The owner was loyal to your father and he's given us his blessing to use it. During the day, you'll need to stay here. Your sleeping routine will have to change for the next few days."

"What sleep?" Aramis said with a chuckle.

"How long before your army arrives?"

"If Lynessa sent them when I asked? Three days, maybe four."

Larson tilted his head and squinted his eyes, muttering calculations to himself.

"If they don't kill or capture the patrols on their way in, Adamar will know they're coming before they get close. The element of surprise will be lost and he'll be prepared to fight. I'll send a runner to pass the word to the army."

"Good idea," Aramis replied. "I honestly hadn't thought of that."

"Well then," Larson motioned toward the ladder. "After you."

They climbed up and opened a grate like the one on the outside of the walls. The grate opened and closed without a sound. *Larson must keep it oiled,* he thought. The night air was warm. The alley they came up into was quiet and dark except for the rats and other denizens of the night that scurried in the shadows.

Larson closed the grate and then motioned for Aramis to follow him. They paused at the end of the alley, then Larson casually stepped out into the main street and glanced around. Satisfied all was clear, he nodded to Aramis. The two walked a block north, toward the castle, and stopped at the building on the corner of the street. A newly painted sign swung above the doorway. It read: *Kingsway Tavern.* Aramis found the name funny in an ironic way.

They entered the building and found that it was empty with the exception of the owner, who stood behind the bar.

"Larson," he greeted with a nod. He was wiping a glass with a rag.

"Albert," Larson replied, "this is Aramis."

Albert set the glass on the counter, tucked the rag into his belt, and came around the bar. He stopped a few feet from Aramis and knelt on one knee.

"My Lord," he said humbly, "as I served your father, so I shall serve you. Anything you require is yours. Merely say the word."

"Thank you, Albert. Please, rise."

Albert stood back up. "Business has been slow lately, so I was just doing some cleaning. Do you need anything?"

"Yes," Aramis answered. "Ink and paper, if you have any."

"Of course." Albert disappeared behind the bar and returned a moment later carrying parchment paper, a quill, and an ink vial.

Larson cleared his throat. "We may want to keep you out of sight. In case anyone decides to come in for a drink."

"Take any room you want," Albert said.

Aramis accepted the items from Albert and headed toward the stairs that led to the rooms. Larson followed. Aramis picked a room at random, checking to make sure it had a desk. He took a seat and began scribbling onto the paper.

"What are you writing?" Larson asked.

"A letter to my brother."

"I'm sorry?"

"He doesn't know where I am. I'm going to send him a letter with false information. I'll need one of your men to deliver it to the castle."

"Do you think that's wise?" Larson asked.

"If we can divert his attention elsewhere, the army can get here with little notice."

"I suppose …"

Aramis finished writing and blew on the ink to make it dry faster. "Can you get someone to deliver it tonight?"

"I'll take care of it," Larson said.

The next morning, while Aramis and Larson were eating, a messenger came into the underground makeshift camp.

"Sir," he said to Larson. His breathing was labored.

Larson stood up. "What is it?"

The messenger shook his head, tried to speak, and fell silent. His eyes became watery.

"What happened?" Larson asked, the worry in his voice evident.

"Dead," was all the man managed to say.

Larson glanced back at Aramis. "I'll be back." He left with the messenger.

Aramis could only guess at what might have happened. He finished his breakfast and then summoned his sword and armor and began practicing his sword fighting. Before he'd left in exile, he would practice with the soldiers. While he wasn't the most skilled, he could certainly handle himself in most situations. And his magical armor and sword didn't hurt either.

A quarter of an hour into his practice, he had worked up a sweat. While his armor was practical, there was only one flaw: ventilation. His body heat was trapped inside the metal encasing, making him burn up more than other types of armor he'd worn. He stopped to drink some water and Larson returned.

"What happened?" Aramis asked between mouthfuls of cold water.

"The messenger who was here. His brother was killed last night. His head was removed and set on a pike outside the castle. His body was hung by the feet above the castle's main gate."

"Gods," Aramis said, shaking his head. "For what?"

"For delivering your message," Larson said softly. "Whatever was in it, your brother did not take it well."

Aramis slumped to the floor, dropping his water. The wooden cup clattered to the floor and the water splashed his legs. "I never ..." he sighed. He opened his mouth several times to speak, but words failed him.

"Don't blame yourself," Larson finally said. "Adamar is a cruel man."

"We cannot use that excuse to justify all of his atrocities," Aramis replied. "This ends. Now."

"Physical might can never compare to the power of Mordum."

—Garrick

CHAPTER 11

Aramis was sprinting toward the castle, his anger overriding his good sense. He'd outdistanced Larson when the man had tried to stop him. The man meant well, but Aramis knew there was only one way to stop Adamar. He had to kill him.

The main gate was shut. Aramis pulled his helm down mid-stride, lowered his head, and ran as fast as he could. He slammed into the gate with the force of an ox, bending the metal barrier and sending it crashing open. Several guards stood nearby. As he breached the walls, they all gaped at the spectacle, unsure of what was happening.

One of them snapped out of the shock and drew his blade, then charged him. Aramis summoned his own blade and met the man head-on. Their blades clashed together loudly. The guard issued a curse. Even with his armor, Aramis felt the vibration in his arm. He fought like a man gone mad, lacking all self-control. His practiced moves and footwork were drowned by his sheer ferocity and wild strikes.

Aramis quickly had the man on the retreat. The man attempted to feign left but slipped on a loose rock and Aramis had him, driving his onyx blade into the man's stomach. He violently ripped the blade free, then met his next attacker.

A peal like thunder shook the courtyard and Aramis realized someone had sounded the alarm. He noticed black robed men streaming from the castle, heading towards him. Pure rage and something darker inside him took over. He howled like an animal and swung his blade in any direction his arm would go. Blood splattered his armor and covered the ground, bathing the stones with a slickness he found hard to navigate.

He hardly noticed the flash of light in the corner of his eye before he felt himself flying through the air. His senses disoriented, he didn't know what was happening even after he crashed hard into the castle wall. Aramis struggled to his feet and was quickly surrounded. His breathing was labored and his muscles burned like fire, but he refused to give in to exhaustion. He swung his sword and severed someone's arm at the elbow. Another swing caught a man in the face, splitting him open from his ear to his cheek.

He saw one of the black robed men standing among the crowd of soldiers that had surrounded him. Aramis lunged toward him and tried to cut him down, but his blade turned at the last moment and struck the ground harmlessly. Aramis growled and swung again with the same result. So focused on trying to strike the man, he was taken completely by surprise when something heavy struck him in the head.

He staggered from the blow and his legs became wobbly. His muscles rebelled against him and he collapsed to the ground.

"Don't touch him!" he heard someone shout. And then he was laying on his back, staring up at the sky. An unfamiliar face knelt over him.

"Impressive, little brother. Though I must admit, it was foolish. Whatever you were trying to attempt ..." Adamar frowned. "Well, let's say it was a wasted effort." Adamar looked to someone who Aramis could not see. "Bind him, gag him, and take him to my quarters. Do not leave him alone. If he escapes, your life is forfeit."

Before Aramis realized he was being lifted, his vision went dark. At first, he thought he had passed out. He quickly realized that someone had placed a sack over his head, as he was fully aware of being moved and could hear his guards talking, though the sound was muffled. A door creaked open and the sack was removed. He found the method of his transport to be ludicrous, considering he had grown up in the castle and knew every room.

He immediately recognized his father's chamber. The terrible memory of his father's assassination flooded him, overwhelming his senses. His guards set him roughly into a chair and bound his arms and legs. One of them grabbed a cloth and forced it into his mouth, then tied it in place. He glared at them.

I'll get free, and I will kill all of you! He screamed the thought in his mind as he struggled to break his bonds. One of the robed men entered the room and came to stand in front of him.

"Dispel the armor," he said. His voice was a deep baritone and didn't fit the face that stared down coldly at him. Aramis hardened his eyes in an attempt to show his disobedience.

"Dispel your armor or I will dispel it for you."

Aramis huffed through his nose. He dared the man to try.

Perhaps knowing Aramis would not be complicit, he touched Aramis's forearm and leaned down, placing his face within inches of Aramis's. "I warned you," he said softly.

An intense pain shot through his body. Had he not been bound to the chair, he would have flailed about wildly and fell to the ground. Unable to move, it made the pain that much harder to bear. A muffled noise was all that escaped him through the gag. Then his armor disappeared in a swirl of hissing mist.

He breathed furiously through his nose as the pain receded. The robed man stood back up and straightened his hood. "Now then," the man said. "Tell me where the bones are."

Aramis bit the cloth in anger and frustration. He refused to be a pawn to Mordum or his servants. The robed man's eyes stared at him intently, studying him.

"I understand," the man said. "You are rebellious by nature. No matter. I shall just have to break your will. I can do it, you know. I have broken many men's minds. It's never an attractive sight, madness. It changes you, makes you into something that is neither human nor animalistic, but something in between. If you force my hand, I will do it."

Aramis knew by the look in the man's eyes that he wasn't lying. He saw darkness in the man's eyes, but not the darkness that had consumed his own. A different darkness, but no less real. Yet he knew if he gave up the location of the bones, any chance of stopping Adamar and Mordum would be impossible. He hardened his gaze. *No,* he thought, *I will not give him anything willingly.*

The man shrugged, turned, and left the room. Aramis looked at the guards. He didn't recognize them. They were probably men his brother recruited. If he could escape his bonds, he knew he could deal with them easily enough. Since his armor was gone, the ropes were not as tight. He kept his eyes on the guards as he began to wriggle his arms, trying to pull his wrists through the ropes. Just as he almost had one arm free, the robed man came back into the room.

He was carrying a glass orb that glowed faintly with a red hue. White tendrils floated around within it, their motions slow and lethargic. There was something about the orb that grabbed his attention. He tried to look away, but he couldn't. His eyes remained fixed on the orb and his thoughts became fuzzy. And then he found himself floating on a sea of red. Wispy clouds floated above him, churning lazily. He felt groggy, as though he had just woken and not gotten enough sleep. Everything around him moved in slow motion.

"Hello?" he called out. The word disappeared into the distance. There was no echo, no reply, nothing. And then he heard the dark whispers. They said terrible things. He covered his ears with his hands to blot out their voices, but it didn't help. The whispers intensified. They sounded angry. They demanded things from him. Things that he knew he shouldn't give them. He fought back against the voices, denying them. That only angered them further.

Suddenly, one of the cloud wisps came for him. It changed direction from the rest of the clouds, moving down towards him. It was slow, but Aramis found that when he tried to move, it was like being stuck in molasses. His movements were sluggish and the cloud easily caught him. It wrapped around his head, but he didn't feel it touch him. And then the things he knew he shouldn't give flew freely from him mind.

"No!" he cried.

The dark whispers laughed. And then he had the sensation of falling.

"What is *he* doing here?" an angry voice demanded.

Aramis blinked several times, trying to clear his mind. Something had happened, but he couldn't remember what. He shook his head, fighting against the fuzziness. The world around him swam momentarily, then came into glaring focus.

The robed man held the orb, but there was no color swirling within it. It was clear and empty. Then he saw his brother, Adamar, for the first time. He stood as tall as Aramis but he was thin by comparison. Fine-boned and long-fingered, he cut a handsome figure in the opulent court clothes that he was wearing. Light blue eyes under long lashes were as pretty as any maiden's, and his classic, even features reminded Aramis of sculptures he had seen. Were it not for his evil actions, Aramis guessed that the ladies of the court would have vied for his attention. Yet for all his beauty, Aramis sensed a vulnerability in him.

"I don't like repeating myself," Adamar said, his tone icy.

"We thought you sent him," one of the guards answered.

The robed man smiled condescendingly. "I was just leaving," he said. He looked to Aramis and tilted his head. "Thank you for the conversation." He started to leave, but Adamar blocked his path.

"What are you doing here?" he asked. "And why do you have that with you?" Adamar pointed at the orb.

"The Prophet asked me to gather some information," the man answered. "And so I have."

"What information?" Adamar demanded.

"I'm afraid I can't say. You can ask the Prophet, if you'd like. I do need to be on my way," the man said. "The Prophet doesn't like to be kept waiting." Adamar stepped out of the way with a growl. The robed man, his face smug, left the room.

"I don't want to see him around this prisoner again. Is that understood?" Adamar's face was flushed red with anger. The guards nodded uneasily.

"Let him hide behind Ilias's power. Once I have gained the Mark, it is *I* who shall rule Mordum's servants!"

No one spoke and no one moved. Finally, Adamar walked over to Aramis and removed the gag. Aramis inhaled deeply, relieved to breath better.

"Tell me, Aramis, why you are here? Certainly, you know that you have signed your own death warrant?"

Aramis studied his brother before answering. "I am here to reclaim the throne that you have stolen."

Adamar laughed. "Stolen? I am the eldest of us. I am the rightful heir to the throne. You are *nothing.*"

Aramis could see that there was a deep-seated rage within Adamar. He wondered what happened to him, wondered what he had experienced to make him full of so much hatred. Aramis knew that anything he said would fall on deaf ears.

"I don't know where you've been all these years," Aramis said, "but I am heir to the throne. It is known to everyone in this kingdom by royal proclamation." Aramis shook his head. "You have no legitimacy other than the *claim* that you are the heir. You have nothing but your word. And the word of a killer is worthless."

Adamar's eyes lit up with a burning fury and Aramis had the fleeting thought that perhaps he'd gone too far. He didn't care. Whether they were brothers by blood or not, Aramis hated him. He'd killed their father and there was nothing that could quell his own hatred for Adamar.

"Leave us!" Adamar shouted. The guards scrambled to flee the chamber. The last one to leave slammed the door shut behind him. Adamar paced back and forth across the chamber in front of Aramis.

"I understand from the Prophet that you are the chosen vessel for Mordum's return," he said as he paced. "Tell me, *brother,* what did you do to catch our dark god's attention?"

"I serve no god," Aramis spat. "Least of all Mordum."

Adamar paused to look at him. "I held the same delusion once," he said. "Over the years, I have learned otherwise." He began pacing again. "The gods do they as please, choosing us for service when they see fit. Assuming you live beyond today … give it time. You'll see things as I do."

"I will never see things as you do. You are a tyrant. I've seen the destruction your troops have brought upon the people. Your people. How could you?" Aramis asked, his voice rising to match his anger that threatened to boil over.

Adamar sighed. "You don't understand, do you? I thought you'd have figured it out by now. Seen the signs." Adamar walked over to a table that sat in the corner, adorned with a few crystal glasses and a bottle of brandy. He poured himself a glass and looked at Aramis from over his shoulder. "Would you like some? The servants found it in the pantry, hidden behind some flour. Apparently, father had a secret stash and was keeping the best stuff for himself."

Aramis glared in response.

Adamar shrugged and downed the entire glass. He refilled the glass and then resumed his pacing. "I'm going to be honest with you. As such, I expect you to do the same service to me. Can you agree to that?"

Aramis remained silent.

"I'll take your silence as consent, then. Where do I start?" he asked aloud. "How about from the beginning, as far I know it to be true. You and I are brothers, but only half. We share the same father, but my mother died after contracting the plague. Father spiraled into a depression after that. A long, deep darkness that consumed him. Have you ever experienced anything like that? I suppose you haven't. But I have." Adamar took a sip from the glass.

"I was ten when death took her from us. She was beautiful. Her passion for life was unrivaled. I think that is what father loved most about her." Adamar paused for a long moment before continuing. When he spoke again, Aramis could hear a strangled emotion in his voice.

"I tried to help him feel better, but nothing worked. The servants told me to be patient, that he needed to grieve and that once enough time had passed, he would find some normalcy. As the years passed, I began to doubt that was true. Those years were difficult, to understate it. I was passed from one servant to another, servants who barely noticed my existence. I was tutored and trained as I should have been, but not having father's attention was …crushing."

Aramis thought he saw Adamar wipe a tear from his eye.

"When I was sixteen, father met your mother. Somehow, she managed to pull him out of his depression. He came alive again, enjoying the things he had forgotten for so long. Well, most of them. Father doted on his second wife the way he never had time to do with me. After a few years, she became pregnant with you. My disdain and jealousy doubled when I heard the news. I was already jealous of your mother for the attention father gave her, attention that I never received.

"The thought of a half-brother getting the charming life I never experienced was too much. When it comes to kings, second sons are … disposable, only needed in the event that the heir dies prematurely. Second sons never feel the weight of the crown, nor the dangers of kingship. I digress." Adamar drank the rest of the brandy and returned the glass to the table.

"Why are you telling me this?" Aramis asked. "Are you trying to justify your evil by blaming our father's grief for your childhood? That it didn't go the way you wanted it to? Please, spare me! That's life. Nothing ever goes the way you plan."

"You are right, my brother. You are too right."

Aramis knew that he should hate Adamar, but he was finding it hard to keep that hatred burning the more he heard.

"Yet I am not trying to justify anything. The things that happened, happened. There was nothing that anyone could have done to change that. But," Adamar came to stand in front of Aramis and looked him in the eyes. Aramis could see that his eyes were watery and red. *Is he crying?* Aramis thought. "father and I didn't agree on many things, least of all ... you. When you were born, the physicians thought you were blind. Your eyes had a milky substance that could not be cured. Father suggested ..."

Adamar sighed and bowed his head. "Father suggested that you be put out of your misery. Since you weren't going to be heir, he felt that he would be doing you a service, keeping you from facing the difficulties of life without sight. I disagreed."

Aramis didn't want to believe it, but ... something in Adamar's tone made him consider the words closely.

"What happened?" Aramis asked.

Adamar looked at him. "I told him you weren't blind. I didn't know for certain, but I thought I had seen your eyes following me a few times. It was only a suspicion, but one that ended up being proven. Unfortunately, it took an action on my part that father found unforgivable."

"What did you do?"

"Nothing to warrant his wrath. I merely committed a few acts that shined an undesirable light on me. Father cared about how people saw him too much. He didn't like the negative attention from what I did, and so … he banished me. That forced him to keep you alive. Thankfully, one of the physicians found a cure for your eyes. It turns out you weren't blind after all."

Wait, Aramis thought. *He …*

"You saved my life?" Aramis asked, his voice a whisper.

"I wouldn't go that far," Adamar said.

"No," Aramis suddenly understood why he'd never heard of his brother. "No, you did save my life. If you hadn't been banished, father would have followed through. I would be dead."

Adamar nodded.

Aramis was overwhelmed with emotions, but then his suspicion returned. "What about what you've done to our people? To our father?"

Adamar knelt in front of him. "Lies, all of it. I would never have father killed. We may not have been close, but he was my father the same as yours. The Prophet, unbeknownst to me, sent an assassin to kill father. I didn't know, I swear it."

"Then why did you claim the throne?"

"The Prophet told me that father had removed my banishment and had requested that I return. He tricked me," Adamar said harshly. "I had no reason to doubt him. When father exiled me, I had nowhere to go. Ilias found me. I was starving, living on the streets in Talvaarin. I fled our kingdom because everywhere I went, people shunned me. No one would give me work. I even begged on the corners for spare coins. People spat on me and cursed me. I …"

Aramis felt himself welling with emotions. Confusion, anger, disappointment. So many that he couldn't fully feel any single one over the other. "I'm sorry," he said. "I'm sorry that you went through that."

"It wasn't your fault," Adamar replied. "I did what I did for the right cause. I never anticipated father banishing me, but that doesn't change why I did what I did. Given the same situation again, I wouldn't choose any differently. The things I experienced helped make me who I am today."

"So, you came here thinking that you were going to be reunited, only to find that father had been killed?"

"Yes," a tear slid down Adamar's cheek. "I arrived after he'd been killed, but before the funeral. I was told that you had killed him. I didn't know you or your character, so I assumed it to be true. I had the guards sweep the city for you. They never found you. I assumed that you had fled, and that was proof of your guilt."

"I was being held as a prisoner in the dungeons," Aramis said. "I was tortured and told to admit that I had killed our father. I didn't kill him, and I refused to admit anything like that."

Adamar stood up. "You were in the dungeon the entire time?"

"Until my friend rescued me."

"Melchiades, right? Yes, I was told he had helped you murder our father." Adamar shook his head in disbelief. "They lied to me," he muttered. "They lied to me!" he repeated, shouting it. "Ilias had our father killed and blamed on it you. I can't believe it. Why would he do that? I trusted him. He was like a second father to me."

"From what I've seen and experienced at the hands of Mordum and his servants, I'm surprised you want the Mark. They are all dark and twisted people."

"No, not all of them," Adamar said. "I've come to see that corruption has indeed filled Mordum's ranks, but it wasn't always like that. Not until recently. Something has changed, but I don't know what. Mordum told me to find you, to keep you safe. The Prophet said Mordum wants to take human form and that he has chosen you as the vessel. You must feel so blessed."

"Blessed?" Aramis said. "Gods, no. I didn't want this blasted mark to begin with. A templar cursed me with it."

"That's odd," Adamar said. "Mordum only gives the mark to those who ask for it. I believe you, but … I don't understand. That's not possible."

"Did they tell you that, too?"

Adamar's shoulders slumped. "I'm sorry, Aramis. If I'd have known they weren't what they said they were …"

"What do we do?" Aramis asked.

"What do you mean?" Adamar replied.

"The man who had the orb. He did something to me. I'm not sure how, but he forced my armor to dispel. And I think he found out where the bones are."

"The bones of Mordum?" Adamar's sudden excitement worried Aramis.

"Yes," he answered. He watched his brother carefully as he related how he got the bones. Adamar was excited, but not in a way that justified his initial worry.

"So, you have the blood and the bones? That is good. I have the ashes. Where are they? We need to keep them out of Ilias's hands."

"The blood is back at my hideaway. The bones are hidden by magic, but I can get them. We may have a problem, though."

"What?"

"The man with the orb. I think he knows how the bones are hidden. I'm a little confused as I think about it, but I think he pulled the information from me. Everything is muddled."

"Then we need to hurry. There are different types of crystal spheres like that, but there are some that can rob a man of his wits. It's possible he used it to get what he wanted out of you. He's probably going to find the bones as we speak."

"Can't you send your men to stop him?"

Adamar shook his head. "He's a higher rank than I am. If my men even obeyed that order, he'd have them killed. No, we've got to do this ourselves." Adamar unsheathed a dagger from the folds of his tunic and cut Aramis's bonds. "He's templar and he's very dangerous. Tell me where the blood is and I will retrieve it. You go get the bones."

"I don't think that's going to work," Aramis said as he stood up. He rubbed his bruised and scraped wrists. "There's a network of men loyal to our father who have it. If they saw you, they would kill first and ask questions later. I'll get them both and bring them to you. Where should we meet?"

Adamar rubbed his chin, thinking. "There's a house in the city. It's secluded and abandoned. I can slip you out of the castle, but the rest is on you."

"What about you?" Aramis asked. "What are you going to do?"

"I'll keep Ilias and the others busy."

"What if they ask where I am?"

"I'll make something up. Don't worry about me. Come on, we've got to hurry." Adamar opened the door to the room and stepped into the hall. Two guards stood on either side of the doorway. "Their prisoner says there is another man here in the castle. Go, find him. Bring him to me alive!"

The guards sprinted off. Adamar walked both ends of the hall to make sure they were alone, then he waved for Aramis to follow him. Adamar led Aramis to the end of the hall and into an empty room on the right side. He closed the door behind him. "There's a passage in this room that leads outside the castle walls. You'll need to find a way back in as the door only opens one way. I'm sure however you got into the city will work for you again. Meet me at the end of District street. You'll know the building when you see it. The windows are boarded."

Adamar pressed a stone and a section of the wall shifted back and to the left, revealing a narrow staircase. Aramis grabbed a torch from the wall. "It was odd finding out I had a brother. I didn't believe it at first. It's even more odd meeting him after all this time." Aramis smiled. "I like it, though. I'll see you in a few hours. Together, we'll stop this darkness before it's too late."

Adamar embraced him in a hug. "Be safe, my brother."

"I will." Aramis nodded, then stepped into the tunnel and disappeared into the darkness. Adamar pressed the same stone and the wall slid back into place.

Mordum was right. That was easy.

—Melchiades

CHAPTER 12

It took Aramis longer to escape the castle than he thought it would. The tunnel branched off in different directions, all leading to caved in chambers or dead ends. By the time he finally found the exit that led outside the city, he had gotten turned around and backtracked several times.

The sun was setting and the sky was painted with beautiful colors. Aramis felt hope for the first time since his father's death.

I have a brother!

The knowledge that his brother was merely deceived and being used by the gods as he was offered some comfort. Finally, someone who understood what it was like to be a pawn in a game you couldn't control. His excitement made him want to rush, but he knew he needed to stay out of sight. Just because his brother was on his side, didn't mean that fighting Mordum's servants would be any easier.

He walked around the outskirts of the castle for half a mile before he found the sewer entrance that Larson had shown him. The grate was wet with fresh waste that had been dumped. Aramis grit his teeth. Even that could not dampen his joy. He lifted the grate and climbed inside. He made his way carefully through the tunnel to the chamber they'd been using as a hideaway. As soon as he stepped into the room, he was greeted by several faces.

"Aramis!"

He turned to see Hannah. His heart fluttered down into his stomach and he realized in that moment just how much he loved her. He embraced her tightly and held her close for a long moment, breathing in her scent and feeling her soft hair and skin. It felt like a dream.

"I'm so glad you're all right," she said. "Larson told us you went to kill Adamar. I was afraid you'd been captured."

"I was," Aramis said, releasing her. "But I escaped."

"How?" Mel asked. He stepped through the small crowd of people.

"Adamar let me go."

Everyone in the room went silent.

"What do you mean?" Larson finally asked.

"He's not what we think he is," Aramis said. "He's been deceived by Mordum's prophet. He's not responsible for any of this."

"My Lord," Mel said gently. "He's trying to subvert you. We know he's responsible. Everything we've seen …" Mel had a troubled look on his face.

"I know how it looks, but he's not the decision maker. He's not behind any of this."

"What about your father?" Larson asked.

"Mordum's prophet tricked him. He sent the assassin, not Adamar. I know it sounds crazy," Aramis said. "But I believe him."

"It is crazy," Mel said. "The fact that you would believe him is even more concerning. Think about it, my Lord. Think. Why would he tell you all that? Why would he let you go? He wants something from you."

"No," Aramis said, shaking his head. "He's telling the truth. I saw it in his eyes. He said we need to keep the blood and the bones out of the Prophet's reach. He's got somewhere safe we can hold them until we defeat the Prophet and his men."

Aramis realized everyone was staring at him as if he'd gone mad. "What?" he asked. "What is it?"

Larson shook his head. "I can't trust the word of someone who willingly follows the god of death. I've seen things that can't be reconciled to this … information."

Aramis was confused. He wished he could take the things he saw and put them into their minds. If only they had seen and heard what he'd seen, they would know. "If you don't believe him, that's fine. That's your choice. But I do, and I am going to take the blood and the bones to him."

Aramis went to grab the wineskin that held the blood. Mel stepped in front of him and placed a hand on Aramis's chest. "My Lord, I can't let you do this. We've worked too hard to get here. We can't just hand everything over to him."

"Of all the people," Aramis said softly. "I would have expected you to back me. Get out of my way. I'll finish this. I'll end this darkness myself."

Mel didn't budge. His eyes were pleading. *He's trying to trick you,* a voice whispered in his head. *He doesn't want you to succeed.*

"Move," Aramis warned. Mel stood resolute. "I said move," Aramis said again. "You can't handle it, can you?"

"I'm sorry?" Mel asked, confused.

"You can't handle the fact that this war is coming to an end. Your entire life's mission has been to fight against Mordum. If he's defeated, you wouldn't know what to do with yourself, would you?"

"My Lord, think about what you are saying. I never wanted war in the first place. Can't you see that Adamar has you fooled? You are going to give him everything he needs to bring Mordum back into this world. *Please*, tell me you see the truth."

Aramis did see the truth. "Move," he said again.

"I cannot let you do this."

Mel's betrayal stung worse than anything he'd ever felt. Aramis's eyes watered with tears. "I knew it," he said. "I knew you would do this, but I thought maybe …" Aramis clenched his jaw and steeled his emotions. "I thought maybe you'd value our friendship more than the lines in the sand. You know I don't want this. But I have no choice."

Aramis pushed Mel away, then summoned his armor and his blade. The air hissed, echoing off the walls of the chamber. The others gathered scrambled out of the way. Hannah backed up, shaking her head in disbelief. "What happened to you?" she asked, horrified.

Her disgust wrenched his heart, but he knew that she didn't understand. He could forgive her of that. Mel stood protectively in front of the wineskin. *That,* Aramis thought, *I can never forgive.*

"Please, my Lord. Aramis," Mel said, shaking his head. "Please don't do this."

"I am your king," Aramis said coldly. "And you will address me as such. Get out of my way or I swear by the gods I will cut you down."

When Mel didn't move, it enraged him. The dark whispers began filling his ears, urging him to strike him down. They told him things that Mel had thought about him. His rage took over and he charged Mel, swinging his blade in a downward chop, seeking to cleave him from shoulder to hip. Mel's surprise was splayed across his face. He managed to summon his own blade in time to block the strike.

Aramis heard Larson and his men draw their own blades. "Traitors, all of you!" he snarled. "You will all regret this!" he screamed. He turned on Larson's men. One of them came at him, waving his sword wildly. Aramis quickly sidestepped and tripped the man as he passed. He tumbled to the ground. Another man began to circle around him, trying to flank him from the rear.

With a growl, Aramis threw himself into the others, kicking, punching and even jabbing with the hilt of his blade. His anger told him to kill them, but something else kept his hand from following through. He knocked several of them unconscious and broke a few noses. Larson dropped his blade, the fear evident on his face.

Aramis turned back towards the wineskin to find Mel still guarding it. He'd summoned his armor and stood in a defensive position. The whispers urged him on. He stabbed forward with his blade, attempting to pierce Mel's armor. Mel knocked his sword aside, but didn't counterattack.

Fine, let him die a coward!

He stepped close to Mel and thrust a few strikes at him, testing his defenses. Mel blocked them all easily. Aramis felt his tattoo burning. The power called out to him. It wanted him to use it, to unleash it against Mel. His anger, the whispers, the call of the Mark ... they overwhelmed his senses. He closed his eyes and unleashed the dark power welling within him. A blast of black lightning shot forth from the tip of his blade, striking Mel in the chest.

Mel staggered back from the force, landing heavily against the table and smashing it. The wineskin fell to the floor but didn't burst. Aramis screamed with all of his might. The dark power flowed out from him and black flames consumed everything near his sword. The cot and the broken table flared, giving birth to a fire. Mel rolled out of the flames and got back to his feet. Still, he would not attack.

Aramis sent a torrent of black flames at Mel, bathing him in a shower of darkness. The fire seemed to have no effect on him. He charged Mel again, this time ramming him with his shoulder. The two went down in a clash of metal. Hannah scream. Aramis ripped Mel's helmet off and punched him in the face several times with his armored fist. Blood splattered his armor and Mel's body went limp.

Aramis got up and walked through the fire he'd created and grabbed the wineskin. He realized Hannah was trapped by the fire. He ran to her and wrapped his body around hers, then stepped through the flames, using his armor as a shield for her. He knew the fire would end up consuming the entire room. He didn't care. He glanced at the men who lay unconscious on the ground. Larson was trying to pull one of them toward the exit tunnel. Mel's body still lay unmoving.

They'll see, he thought. *In this life or the next, they will see I was right.*

He led Hannah out of the burning chamber using the ladder that led into the alley above. She was shaking uncontrollably. Aramis reached out to touch her face and she flinched. He drew his hand away. *So be it.*

She met his eyes briefly. He smiled at her, but he could see the fear in her eyes. He'd become something else entirely to her. She would see. She would see just like the others would see.

He left her in the darkened alley, alone. He dismissed his armor and blade as he walked toward District street.

● ∞ ● ∞ ●

Aramis found the house easily enough. It was the only building on the street that seemed out of place. Everything else was in good condition and well taken care of. The boarded windows hid any light that might be shining within.

The door was unlocked and opened with a soft creak. The main room was alight with a fire burning in a stone hearth. The walls showed signs of age and the floor squeaked as he made his way toward the figure standing in front of the fire.

"Brother," he called out.

"Aramis," Adamar replied. "Did you bring the items?"

"I brought the blood."

Adamar turned from the fire to face him. "What of the bones? Did the templar get them?"

"No," Aramis said. "They are still hidden by the spell. I can get the magic to release them anywhere I am."

Adamar stared at him. "What happened? You look like you ran to get here."

"It's nothing," Aramis answered with a shrug. "It doesn't matter."

Aramis knelt on the floor and drew his rusty dagger. He cut a circular shape into the wood and crossed through it with an intricate set of lines. After he finished, he sheathed his dagger and closed his eyes. Feeling the power of the Mark flowing through him, he channeled it toward the symbol he'd cut. The air rippled in front of him briefly before a brown sackcloth appeared. Cutting off the flow of power, he snatched the bag up just as the symbol burst into flames. They seared the floor and then quickly diminished.

"The Mark gives you magic?" Adamar asked curiously.

"No. Well, not that I know of. The spell was cast by a wizard. She told me how to unlock it."

Adamar eyed him greedily. "I've begged Mordum for the Mark," he said softly. "Yet he makes me wait for it."

"You shouldn't want it," Aramis replied. "It's brought me nothing but death."

"So where is the blood?"

Aramis produced the wineskin from his belt.

"The blood, the bones, and the ashes," Adamar said with awe. "I knew it would be me. I knew I would be the one to perform the ritual and bring him back."

"What are you talking about?" Aramis said. "We're hiding these from the Prophet until we can kill him. Then we need to find a way to destroy them."

Adamar laughed. "No, little brother. I will not keep Mordum from what he desires. I couldn't even if I wanted to."

Aramis took a step back towards the door. "I am going to stop the plague that is Mordum from spreading."

"I don't think you are going anywhere," Adamar said.

Rough hands grabbed him from behind. He dropped the wineskin and the bag as he struggled against his attackers. He saw a glint of steel and then felt a stinging pain on his arm. He managed to glimpse his arm and saw that his tattoo had been cut.

"Hurry," Adamar commanded. "The Mark will heal. Get him to the ceremony. Quickly!"

Aramis was struck in the back of the head and then there was only darkness.

"To abandon a friend to the darkness would be an assault upon my conscience."

—Melchiades

CHAPTER 13

When he awoke, the first thing he noticed was the noise. Hundreds of people, most of them wearing the robes of Mordum's priests, were gathered around a large pit that had been dug. Aramis guessed it must have been created recently, as the dirt was dark and fresh.

The crowd was chanting, but he couldn't make out the words. The ringing in his ears was hindering him from making out their words. He also had a pounding headache. He was standing upright, bound by thick ropes across his legs and chest. Aramis tested their strength. They didn't budge. He tried to summon his blade, but nothing happened. The connection he felt to the Mark was nonexistent. Glancing down, he saw why.

His tattoo had been cut and the skin was pinned back, keeping the two pieces from touching. *Disgusting,* he thought. The way his arms were tied, he couldn't reach to remove the small metal pins. He looked up. He was standing atop a raised platform in front of the pit, overlooking the crowd. It was like looking at a sea of blackness. There were hundreds, if not thousands, of the robed men. All of them followers of Mordum.

Aramis cursed them under his breath. He listened intently to their chanting. He could only hear it faintly above the ringing, but he could swear that the words were calling to him. He grew uncomfortably warm. Something was happening, but he didn't know what. The crowd continued their chant, and Aramis suspected they were saying the same words, over and over.

The sky filled with storm clouds. They came suddenly, with incredible speed. Solid black, roiling and churning like some sort of monster. The clouds devoured the tops of the castle's guard towers, crawling over them to consume them whole. The chill wind strengthened, whipping dust from the ground into eyes and mouths.

A bolt of lightning flashed out from the clouds above, spearing the ground near the pit. Thunder exploded. The concussion knocked some of the priests to the ground. A small group of women screamed. The men who were still standing tried to calm them, but the women would have none of it. They fled in a mad panic.

"Forget them!" Adamar shouted from beside Aramis. He wondered if his brother had been there the whole time, or if he had just arrived.

The storm clouds raced across the sky, battling the sunlight, defeating it easily. The sun fell, overcome by darkness. Night was upon them, a night thick with swirling dust. Aramis could see nothing, not even his own feet. The next second all around him was illuminated by another devastating lightning bolt. Rain slashed sideways, coming at him all like arrows fired from a million bowstrings. Hail pounded on him like iron-tipped flails, cutting and bruising. Lightning walked among the crowd, casting its flaming spears. Thunder shook the ground and roared.

The rain fell harder, if that were possible. Aramis wondered how long the raging storm could last. It felt like a lifetime, like he had been born in the storm and would grow old and die in the storm. The rain and ice pelted him and felt like stinging nettles across his entire body. He could only lower his head to try and shelter his face, but even that seemed futile.

A lightning flash momentarily blinded him. The blast deafened him. The force of the thunderbolt lifted a man off his feet and slammed him back down. The bolt had struck so close, Aramis could hear the sizzle in the air and smell the phosphorous and sulfur. He could also smell burnt flesh. As his sight slowly restored, he looked in the direction of the man who'd been struck. The priest's flesh glowed red beneath a black crust, like a hunk of overcooked meat. Smoke rose from it; the wind whipped it away, along with flecks of charred flesh. The skin of the man's face had burned away, revealing a mouthful of hideously grinning teeth.

Adamar braved the wind and rain and leapt down from the platform, landing at the edge of the pit. He grabbed a sack from one of the cowering priests and climbed down into the pit. From Aramis's vantage point, he could barely make out what his brother was doing. Adamar reached into the sack and pulled out something white—bones. He lay them out, piecing them together until it looked like a skeletal man lay in the dirt. Then he pulled the wineskin out of the sack and poured the blood on the bones. He covered the skull with it and even kneeled to smear it, ensuring the entire skull was covered. Then he pulled out a small box and dumped out what Aramis assumed were the ashes.

The wind died. The rain softened to a steady downpour. The hail ceased altogether. Thunder rumbled a drumroll, which seemed to mark time with the pace of a strange figure of darkness steadily growing nearer with each illuminating flare. The storm receded, carrying its fury to the other side of the castle, to other parts of the world.

Soaking wet, Aramis shook the water and muck from his face. The wind was cold and crisp and chill, and he was shivering. The dark cloud filled the pit, obscuring Adamar within its clutches. Slowly, yet steadily, it flowed forth out of the pit, coming towards the platform, towards Aramis. An intense feeling of dread spread through him. He struggled against his bonds again, but they wouldn't give way.

The shadowy cloud pooled onto the platform at his feet, gradually shifting and turning until a vague outline of a man formed. The face was insubstantial and shifted amongst itself, never staying the same. Despite that, Aramis knew exactly what—who—stood before him.

"Mordum," he whispered.

The form pulsed in recognition of its name. Suddenly the pins in his arm came loose and clattered to the ground. His skin rolled back together, healing by the power of the mark. Heart thudding against his chest, Aramis stared into the face of darkness, the face of death. And then the shadow plunged into his mouth.

● ∞ ● ∞ ●

Adamar climbed out of the pit just as the shadowy cloud that was Mordum entered Aramis's body. He watched in envy while Aramis's body twitched and jerked as Mordum fought for control. Suddenly, a horn split the air. Adamar looked from tower to tower to see who was sounding the alarm. Spotting a guard waving a flag, he ordered one of the priests to go find out what was happening.

He turned his attention back to Aramis. His younger brother writhed and his eyes rolled into the back of his head. "He's putting up a stronger fight than I expected," he muttered to himself.

A tremor shook the ground, following quickly by another. The horn sounded again, this time from the other side of the courtyard. A whistling sound filled the air. Adamar looked in every direction, but he didn't see anything. A crashing sound echoed through the air.

"What is going on?" Adamar demanded angrily. The priests were standing around confusedly. They began to murmur among themselves. "I have to do everything myself, it seems." Adamar pushed through the crowd toward the first guard tower he'd spotted that had been sounding the alarm. As he got closer, it was evident something was wrong. Soldiers were running towards the main gate, hauling long timbers.

"My Lord," a breathless soldier hailed him. "Creatures," he gasped. He placed his hands on his knees and bent over, trying to restore his breath. Adamar waited impatiently while trying to get a view beyond the gate.

"Forgive me," the man finally said. "There are creatures attacking the gate. I've never seen the like before. The others are trying to fortify the damage from earlier." The soldier's eyes strayed towards Aramis and the pit.

"Creatures? What do they look like?" Adamar asked.

Metal clanged as the gate shuddered inward. Shouts and curses rose from the soldiers who were trying to brace the damaged gates. Adamar stalked to the crowd of soldiers, leaning left and right to try and see what creatures were attacking his castle. And then he caught sight of one of them, just barely. Its head was large and round and looked like a stone.

"Golems," a voice said. Adamar turned to see his remaining body guard standing beside him.

"What?" Adamar said, wondering where his guard had disappeared to. "I've never heard you speak before," he added.

"Golems," the templar said. "They are creatures formed of magic and earth. There are few who can summon them."

Adamar looked back at the gate. "How do you kill them?" he asked.

"You must kill the one who summoned them," the templar answered.

"What are you waiting for?" Adamar demanded. "Go deal with them!"

The templar wavered for a brief second before bowing and leaving. The hesitation was not lost on Adamar. *What,* he wondered, *could give a templar pause?* As far as he knew, nothing could stop Mordum's most powerful servants. Perhaps the templar was not used to fighting solo. The blasted Prophet of Edria has killed his other templar guard and Mordum had not answered his call for a replacement. He pushed his doubts from his mind.

"My Lord," the priest from the crowd jogged over to him. "There are creatures attacking the gate."

"So I've seen," Adamar said, his annoyance plain.

"To the west, a large army is approaching."

"How large?" Adamar asked.

"I think you'll want to see for yourself," the priest answered.

"Show me."

The priest led him across the courtyard to a curved stone stairway that led upwards to the battle ramparts. They climbed the flight of stairs quickly and Adamar saw a trio of soldiers pointing in the distance.

"Let me see," Adamar growled. He took the spyglass from one of the soldiers. *If that priest is exaggerating ...*

Lifting the device to his right eye, he gazed out across the plains and scanned the horizon. At first, he didn't see anything. Then he noticed a plume of dust. He followed its length until he found the source. A black mass encompassed his view. He tried adjusting the device, but he only made the image blurry.

"Someone fix this thing!" he shouted in frustration. The soldier he'd taken it from adjusted it and handed it back to him. This time, the image was clearer.

Cavalry. Hundreds, if not thousands, were riding straight toward him. His hopes soared as he thought they were more of Mordum's mercenaries, but his hope quickly turned to surprise when he saw the banner being carried at the front of the army.

The flag of Keswick.

Adamar clenched his jaw and threw the spyglass. It clanged as it struck the stone.

"Orders, my Lord?"

Adamar's thoughts went rampant. An army marching on him. Creatures at his doorstep. Mordum would soon fully possess his brother, if he hadn't already. He needed to hold them off.

"Ready the catapults. As soon as the army is within distance of the walls, rain hell on them."

He left the wall, taking the stairs two at a time. He ran towards the pit. Climbing onto the platform, he noticed Aramis's body had gone slack and pale. Turning his attention to the crowd of milling priests, he shouted, "To arms!"

The priests glanced askance at one another, obviously confused.

"An army approaches! We must hold them off until our dark lord has taken his vessel. Quickly!"

Adamar knew he might be pressing his luck. Although it was known that he was favored among Mordum's servants, his official rank was not very prestigious. The Prophet himself was likely among the crowd.

In a display that Adamar found truly beautiful, the horde of priests threw back their hoods and summoned their armor and blades. The hissing of mist overpowered any other sound, including the clanging of the gates. A sea of shiny blackness filled his vision and pride swelled within him. This would be *his* army soon.

"To the west!" Adamar shouted as loud as he could. The legion of priests streamed forth, heading to the gates.

He turned to Aramis. It didn't look like he was breathing. *Good,* he thought. *If Aramis is dead, then Mordum is in control.*

Everything was going in his favor. Aramis was dead, the priests were following his commands, and soon Mordum would walk in his midst. Mordum would bless him with the Mark and he would be the new Prophet. All his sacrifice, everything he had worked for, had led to this moment. He shook visibly with excitement.

The clash of steel and the shouts of battle erupted nearby. Adamar turned his attention to the raucous. A small band of men, perhaps thirty of them, were clashing with his soldiers less than a hundred feet away. Adamar looked to the gate, but the creatures had not breached it. In fact, the priests swarmed the gate, pushing it outward and attacking the stone golems.

How in Mordum's name did they get in here?

Drawing his own sword, he leapt off the platform and ran to join the fray. As he neared the battle, he recognized one of the men as Aramis's priest-friend. He'd heard the rumors of the man. Supposedly, he was a priest of Edria before she was killed. If that were true, then his armor and blade had left him. He would be an easy kill.

Adamar charged into the fight, bringing his sword in a downward arc toward the priest. He immediately regretted it as soon as he'd engaged the man. From afar, he appeared to wear normal armor. But as he stood before him now, he realized that the priest still had god blessed armor. He tried to retreat.

"Come now," Mel called after him. "You aren't very brave without your templar guards, are you? Come, let's dance."

Adamar sprinted away, fleeing the battle altogether. He could hear booted steps of pursuit. He ran towards the platform, desperately hoping Mordum had gained full control of Aramis's body. As he clambered on, he risked a glance over his shoulder and saw the priest had been intercepted by his soldiers.

His stomach dropped when he saw that Aramis's body was gone. The ropes lay at the base of the stone slab. He whirled around, bracing for battle. Yet Aramis was nowhere to be seen. Another horn, this one different than the last two, split the air. Adamar looked from the empty slab towards the gate where the priests were swarming out into the main city. Biting his lip in indecision, he left the platform and made his way back to the battle ramparts.

The soldiers were gone, but the spyglass lay where he left it. Snatching it up, he checked to see if it had broken. The only damage was a few scuff marks on the metal. The lens was still intact. He looked out at the advancing army. They were closing on the main city gates. Black armored priests were forming into ranks outside the city, preparing for close quarters battle.

Figuring out how to adjust the device, he turned it to the gates. Large piles of stone lay strewn about. He grinned triumphantly, knowing his templar had found those responsible for the creatures. The last of the priests filtered out of the gates, rushing toward their fellows outside the city. A thunderous boom filled the air and drew Adamar's attention. Flashes of light coming from the approaching army crackled to life, forking their way toward the ranks of Mordum's priests.

The magical lightning shattered upon an unseen barrier. Black flames erupted from the priests and spread across the distance, striking the cavalry. Both men and horses were consumed by the unholy fire. Screams of agony reached Adamar's ears.

He grimaced. He had seen battle before and had even killed. And despite his loyal devotion to the god of the dead, he found that he just couldn't stomach the sounds of the dying. Perhaps it was because they reminded him of his own impermanence. He knew then, in that very moment, that he was afraid to die.

Adamar shook his head to clear his mind. There would be time to think of such things, but it was not now. The enemy was almost to the formation of priests and then the battle would be on in full force.

He imagined what the priests might be feeling. Their hearts pounding, adrenaline coursing through their veins. They stood foot to foot, packed tightly together, with not much room to maneuver. The less space between them, the less of a chance a horseman had to get through. Seconds felt like eternity. And then the army washed up against the line priests. The noise and commotion was loud and rumbling. Adamar stood straight-backed, his chin high. He turned his gaze away from the clashing armies and up to the sky above them. It was dull and gray.

An explosion rocked the ground outside the city. Both sides were thrown into silence. Adamar used the spyglass to see what was happening. Some sort of magical blast had killed hundreds of his priests and soldiers. Their bodies lie smoldering on the field.

The smoke cleared to reveal two forms, both clothed in white robes. Their faces shined brilliantly and Adamar had to look away, lest he be blinded.

"Wizards," he growled under his breath.

"No," a voice beside him said. It startled Adamar and he turned to see Aramis beside him. His hand went to the pommel of his sword, but Aramis raised his hand and Adamar was paralyzed. He couldn't even move his eyes.

Aramis looked to him and Adamar knew that it was not his brother inside the body. Not anymore.

"They are not wizards," the undead voice said. "They are gods."

Had Adamar been in control of his body, he would have given his lord an incredulous look.

"It is time, though I am not ready," Aramis said. He lowered his hand and Adamar's paralysis faded. He fell to his knees.

"My Lord Mordum," he said in a trembling voice. "Grant me the blessing of your Mark. I beg you."

Aramis, or Mordum as he had become, looked down at Adamar. "I do not have the strength to spare," he answered. "Rise, and tell me what is happening now. These eyes are not like my own."

Adamar rose and looked out at the battle. The priests in the rear echelons were already streaming back through the city gates. Many had no idea where they were going, only that they wanted to be far away from the blood and the death.

"My—your," he quickly corrected himself, "priests are fleeing. They are retreating through the gates. Our enemy has routed us!"

"They need a leader," Mordum said calmly. He looked at Adamar and began to whisper words his mortal ears could not hear, then he pointed to where the priests were fleeing. Adamar's body rose into the air and flew over the castle walls towards the battle.

Adamar felt his stomach do strange things as the wind clawed at him. The clouds parted. A mote of sunlight fell from the heavens and touched him as he descended onto the battle field.

"To me!" he shouted. "Rally to me!"

He blazed as if dipped in flame, lit from above with the light. His shout brought the fleeing priests and soldiers to a halt. They looked to see where the call came from and saw Adamar outlined in flame, blazing like a beacon fire. Mordum's servants halted in their mad dash, looking up, dazzled.

"To me!" Adamar yelled again.

The soldiers hesitated, then one ran to him. Another followed and another, glad to have purpose and direction once again.

"Get into formation!" he ordered.

The soldiers and priests came running back, bringing their weapons to bear and lining back up. Adamar felt glorious. Mordum had used him to stop the retreat. All the men's eyes were on him now. *Now who is important?* He cried at them in his mind. *I am!*

"Charge!" he screamed.

His army charged forth, clashing into the ranks of their enemy. He stood still as they flowed around him, watching the death and destruction that ensued. The air begun to buzz. Adamar looked up to see a wave of arrows, hundreds of them, flying toward his position. His eyes widened in terror. He looked back to Mordum, issuing a silent prayer for protection. Yet his lord was nowhere to be seen.

The arrows rained down around him. The feathered shafts struck through visors of helmed soldiers or took them in the throat. More arrows flew, more bodies fell. The panic-stricken soldiers and priests faltered, halted, trying to discover the location of this new enemy. More arrows hummed through the air. Men screamed and fell.

The dying were starting to pile up like hideous cordwood in the cut, forming a blood-soaked barricade.

Adamar cursed as the enemy crashed through his forces. He ripped one of the arrows from a fallen soldier and eyed the feathers. The colors were familiar. And etched into the wood was the symbol he least wanted to see: a phoenix bursting from a pile of ashes. The symbol of Talvaard.

The ground trembled beneath his feet. He spun around and spotted the source. One of the golems was coming straight for him. He turned to run, overcome with fear. And then something hit him in the left eye. His mind screamed that he needed to run, but his body screamed in agony and would not obey. His right eye barely recognized the feathered shaft that was lodged in the left before he had the sensation of falling. He crashed to the ground on his back, his head striking something hard. He told himself that should have hurt, yet he felt nothing.

The golem came into his blurred view. His eye was welling uncontrollably with tears. He tried to blink them away and only felt the right side of his face. *What's happening to me?!* his mind screamed. His heart was pounding furiously against his chest and his ears were ringing. He watched as the golem lifted its leg to step on him. He was powerless to move.

A wave of heat washed over him as a blinding streak of light struck the golem in the side of its head. The stone creature turned to face a new attacker and Adamar lay there, giving silent thanks to whoever had just saved his life. He knew he couldn't stay where he was, yet his body refused to cooperate with his commands. He didn't know how much time passed as he struggled to roll onto his side, but eventually he managed to do so.

He lay there, expended, watching the battle continue to unfold. It was hard to tell who was winning. The bodies of both sides littered his view. He tried to get up, but he was dizzy and couldn't keep his balance.

So, he crawled. It was arduous and tiring. His hands touched blood and dismembered limbs, yet he struggled on. He didn't know where he should go. Nowhere was safe. Mordum had abandoned him. Everything had fallen apart so quickly. Every so often, his arms faltered and he lowered himself to the ground. He had to turn his head to keep the arrow from lodging any further into his skull.

Though he wanted to give in many times, he continued onward.

—Prince Aramis

CHAPTER 14

The combined forces of Keswick and Talvaard pushed Mordum's forces into the city. With the gods Zevea and Tael leading the charge, the priests of Mordum fell to blade and magic alike. The army pushed its way into the main courtyard of the castle. Standing there, alone, was a man.

Zevea and Tael closed in, approaching cautiously. Though it was Aramis's body, they knew who really stood before them.

"So, we finally meet in the flesh," Zevea said.

"Why have you come here?" Mordum asked.

"You know why," Tael answered. "What you are doing is forbidden."

"Yet here you both are, in mortal bodies as I am."

"This is different," Zevea said. "We have left our celestial home to stop you."

"My power is greater than yours, and grows by the minute," Mordum laughed. "Kill my servants as you will. Even in death, they still serve me."

"We will crush you," Tael said. "We should have killed you when you were weakened after your first attempt to take this world for yourself."

"You couldn't kill me before, and you can't kill me now."

The gods eyed each other in silence. Tael was the first move. He charged Mordum, swinging a large battleax in an 'X' pattern. Mordum stood still until Tael was a few feet away, then dove down and rolled, coming up behind Tael and slashing him across the back with his onyx blade. Mordum immediately turned to meet Zevea's attack. She wielded a metal staff and struck at his head.

Mordum easily deflected her attempt and spun towards her, slashing a long gash down her arm. She cried out in pain, something foreign to her, and brought her staff around to block Mordum's second strike. Her wound was deep and she was bleeding profusely. The arm was almost useless.

Tael tackled Mordum and the two went crashing to the ground. They wrestled and rolled around, fighting furiously. Zevea wanted to strike Mordum with her staff, but the two were rolling around too much for her to risk hitting Tael.

A thunderous blast rattled the ground. Zevea struggled to see what was happening. Tael stood up, a smile upon his face. "We are vic—" bloody spittle flew from his mouth and he staggered before falling to his knees. A look of surprise spread across his face as his hand touched the mortal wound in his chest.

Zevea felt fear for the first time. She watched as Mordum rose and calmly walked to Tael, easily swinging his blade and removing Tael's head. Blood spurt and the head tumbled to the ground, followed by his headless body. Zevea screamed. First her sister, and now Tael. Mordum, she knew, would never be satisfied.

She tried to grip her staff in both hands, but her cut arm was numb. She backed up slowly as Mordum came towards her.

A flash of silver caught her attention and she saw Melchiades rushing Mordum. It was suicidal.

Mordum turned and met the priest with a flourish of his sword. Their blades clashed together and sparks flew.

"Leave Aramis's body, now!" Mel yelled at him.

Mordum laughed as he parried Mel's strikes. "This body is mine now. Aramis is gone."

"I don't believe you," Mel growled. He fought furiously, trying every maneuver he knew to get close to Mordum, but the god was too quick.

"Are you really going to kill Aramis?" Mordum taunted.

"You said he was gone," Mel cried.

"Perhaps he is, perhaps he isn't. I suppose you will never know."

Mel knew that Mordum was trying to confuse him. He believed Aramis was alive. Somewhere deep inside, he was sure, Mordum held his friend's soul prisoner. He tried to keep his mind focused on the battle, but he kept thinking to what Aramis had told him. Mordum could not be defeated by sheer force or a killing blow. There were specifics. And unfortunately, Aramis had only divulged some of the details. He was already tired. His muscles screamed at him, burning intensely. He couldn't keep up the fight. And this time, there would be no welcoming goddess to give him his life back.

Mordum rushed him, trying to end the fight quickly. Mel blocked the god's charge with his shoulder and his armor cracked from the blow. From his peripheral, he saw Zevea flinch as if in pain. Could she feel what was happening to his armor?

The courtyard began to fill with soldiers. Mel tried to keep his attention on Mordum, but he did notice Garrick. *Where did the man's loyalties truly lie?* he wondered.

His answer came quickly as Garrick joined the fray. His black armor and sword glinted faintly in the dull light of the sun. He attacked Mordum.

The god turned angrily towards Garrick and without a word or movement, Garrick cried out in agony and collapsed to the ground, clutching his chest.

"How dare you?" Mordum thundered. His voice echoed off the castle walls of the courtyard, deep and booming.

Mel saw an opening and charged Mordum, stabbing his blade into the god's side, between his ribs. Mordum turned and punched Mel in the side of his face, sending him reeling. He lost his grip on his sword and fell hard onto his back. Mordum towered over him, raising his own sword for the killing blow.

An arrow slammed into the side of Mordum's head, exploding with magical sparks. Both Mel and the god turned to see Lynessa, the Lady of Keswick. She stood a few feet away, holding a bow. She was surrounded by several priests in gleaming silver armor. Mel recognized them as Zevea's servants. Lynessa nocked another arrow and drew the string back, pointing it at Mordum.

"Release Aramis," she said.

Mordum laughed.

"Your army has been routed and you are outnumbered. God or not, I like my odds better than yours."

"Foolish mortals!" Mordum bellowed. "I am God of the Dead! I cannot die!"

The gray clouds above began to darken. The wind picked up. Lightning flickered in the growing darkness above them and thunder filled the air.

Mel knew that if they didn't kill Mordum now, he would come back again. He would continue to bring death and destruction upon the people. He looked to Zevea.

She was pale and weak. He could sense that she was dying, could feel it in his armor. It wouldn't be long before his tie to her power was severed and he would be without his armor and blade.

The dagger ... her voiced filled his mind, weak and barely a whisper.

Dagger?

The one I gave to Aramis. It is more than it seems ... it can kill him.

Mel looked at Aramis's body and saw it sheathed at his waist. How could a rusty old dagger kill a god?

Trust me, she bade him.

Mel looked to Lynessa and gave her a hand signal. He didn't know if she saw it or not, but there was nothing else to be done. He pushed himself onto his feet and reached for the dagger. Mordum began to turn and face him, but another of Lynessa's explosive arrows struck him in the chest. The concussive force threatened to push Mel backwards, but he dug his boots into the dirt for leverage and forced himself forward. He snatched the blade from Aramis's belt and jabbed the rusty dagger into Mordum's chest, his aim true.

The blade pierced his heart.

The hilt of the dagger became red-hot and burned Mel's hand. He cried out and let go of the blade in shock. His armor began to dissipate, but he couldn't take his eyes off Mordum. The dagger glowed with a blinding white light, piercing the darkness within Aramis's body. The blackness in his friend's eyes dimmed, slowly returning to their natural color.

Aramis's mouth opened in a silent scream and the black cloud that was Mordum rushed out, disintegrating into the air. Aramis's body collapsed lifelessly to the ground. The dagger's glow dimmed and then faded entirely.

Mel rushed to his fallen friend and pulled the dagger out. Aramis was pale and didn't appear to be breathing.

"No," he whispered over and over. "Please, no." Tears stung his eyes. Had he killed his friend by killing Mordum? He looked to Zevea. Her body lay not far, but she was faintly moving.

Come ... she called out to him.

Overcome with grief, he could barely comprehend the word. He forced himself to move and went to her. He wiped his tears. The life was quickly fading from her eyes. She opened her mouth to speak, but no words came out.

You ... can ... save him.

"How?" Mel cried. "Please, tell me how!"

Zevea closed her eyes. *Come near ...*

Mel lowered his head to her, inches from her face. She opened her mouth and breathed out a golden wisp of air. He gasped when he saw it, and the wisp flew into his mouth. He was filled with a tremendous power.

Breath into ...

And then her presence was gone.

Mel stood there, not sure what she intended to say. Panic filled him. She said he could save Aramis, but he didn't know what she was going to say. He fell to his knees at Aramis's side, tears streaming down his face. He turned his friend's face to face him and stared into his lifeless eyes. Agony wrenched his heart. He began to sob uncontrollably. He placed his head on his friend's shoulder. He would have prayed, but he knew there were no gods left to hear him. Lynessa knelt on the other side of Aramis and Mel saw that she too was crying.

Mel raised his head, looking at her. "Why?" he cried. The golden wisp flew out of his mouth. Lynessa's façade of strength broke and she shook her head.

"I—"

The wisp flew into her mouth. Her eyes widened in surprise. She had felt the power, Mel knew. She looked down at Aramis and shook her head again. Leaning down, she pressed her lips against Aramis's in a soft kiss. As she exhaled over him, the wisp slipped out of her mouth and into Aramis's.

Mel saw it and wondered what it could mean. Time passed and Mel dared not move lest he miss something. Lynessa eventually rose to her feet and walked away. Garrick knelt beside Mel and placed his hand on his shoulder.

"We should probably move his body," Garrick suggested quietly. "He paid the ultimate sacrifice. We should honor him for that."

Mel ignored him. Eventually Garrick left, too.

I should never have left him, Mel grieved in his mind. *I should have followed him. Even though Adamar tricked him, I should never have let him out of my sight.*

And then he thought he saw Aramis's chest rise. It was almost imperceptible, and Mel doubted whether he actually saw it. Then his chest rose and fell. Mel wiped his eyes, wanting to be sure of what he saw.

He wasn't seeing things! Aramis was breathing.

"He's alive!" Mel cried out. "He's breathing! Someone help me!"

Garrick and Lynessa rushed to help, followed by others. They lifted him gently and carried him inside the castle. Mel led them to Aramis's room and they laid him on the bed. Lynessa ordered everyone to leave except Garrick and Mel. The three of them took turns watching him while the other two dozed off.

Three days passed uneventfully.

"I'm afraid I must go," Garrick said on the third day, breaking the long silence. "I don't want to, but my duties cannot be ignored much longer."

Mel nodded. "I understand," he replied. "When he wakes, I will tell him you were here."

"Thank you," Garrick said.

"No," Mel shook his head. "Thank you. For honoring your word to him. And for risking your life. Standing up to Mordum like you did ..."

Garrick shrugged. "I don't know how I did it," he said.

They stood quietly as they stared at Aramis's body, still except for his breathing.

"I will come check on him after I have things in order," Garrick said.

Mel nodded and Garrick left the room. Mel was surprised that Lynessa would not leave Aramis's side. Another day passed before there was a change in Aramis.

"Water," a voice woke Mel. He rose from the chair he was sleeping in and saw that Aramis had his eyes open.

"Water," Aramis rasped again.

"Thank the goddess!" Mel exclaimed. He rushed to pour a glass of water from a carafe the servants had left, almost spilling it in his excitement. Bringing the cup to Aramis, he helped hold it while Aramis struggled to lift his head up to take a drink.

Aramis fell back against the pillow. His eyes shifted back and forth across the room. "Where ..."

"We're in the castle. This is your room," Mel answered. "How are you feeling?"

Aramis moved his head weakly to the side so that he could look at Mel. "I feel like death," he whispered. "Mordum?" he asked.

"Dead," Mel said solemnly. "And we nearly lost you as well."

"How?" Aramis rasped.

"We'll get to that when you are better. You should rest."

Aramis's eyes slowly closed and his breathing slowed. Mel watched worriedly, but soon realized Aramis had fallen asleep. He looked up as Lynessa rose from the chair she had been sleeping in.

"What's going on?" she asked.

"Aramis was awake," Mel answered with a smile. "He spoke a little, but I told him to rest."

"Oh, thank Zevea," she whispered.

"I couldn't say it any better," Mel said.

Aramis slept through the rest of the day, waking as dinner was being brought in by the servants. Having regained a small amount of strength, Aramis was able to sit up. The three of them ate together in silence until Aramis spoke.

"I feel like I've been trapped in a dream," he said. His voice was stronger.

"The last few days have felt like a nightmare," Lynessa said quietly.

"How long have I been out?"

"Almost four days if you count today," Mel answered. "It's good to see you awake. I was afraid ..." he left the sentence unfinished.

"My body feels like it fell down a mountain," Aramis said, rubbing the muscles in his right arm. "What happened? All I remember is the storm, and then ... it's all foggy after that."

Mel took a deep breath and related everything, pausing hesitantly when he got to the part where he stabbed Aramis in the chest.

"How am I alive?" Aramis asked.

"Zevea," Mel replied. "She did something. She gave you a breath of air, but it was … different. I can't explain it."

Aramis was surprised. The goddess had saved his life? All the anger he felt toward the gods hadn't left, but maybe he could forgive them in time.

"Where is she?" he asked. "I should probably thank her."

"She's dead," Mel said, the sadness in his eyes evident. "Mordum dealt her a mortal wound. He also killed Tael. Zevea helped you with her dying breath."

Aramis digested the words. "If the gods are dead," he said, "then we have no one to rely upon but ourselves. Just how life was before all of this."

"Well," Mel paused, "there are other gods, though I don't think they meddle in the affairs of men as much."

Mel glanced to Lynessa. "There's something else," he said. He looked back to Aramis. "I didn't get the chance to tell before, when you …" he trailed off.

"Lost my wits?" Aramis finished for him, smiling wanly.

"I would have said it a bit more pleasant, but yes. We found Lord Bavol."

Aramis raised his eyebrows. "Where is he? Is he all right?"

"No," Mel said. "He was dead. Murdered, by the looks of it. By Mordum's orders, no doubt. And you know we found Hannah."

Aramis closed his eyes and bowed his head. "I'm sure she must hate me."

"No," Mel answered. He motioned to one of the servants and then left the room in a rush.

"What of Adamar? Is he dead?"

"I'm afraid I don't know," Mel said. "We haven't found his body. He's just … gone."

A moment later, the servant returned with Hannah following closely behind her.

"Aramis!" she shouted. She ran to the bed and jumped onto it, wrapping her arms around Aramis. Weakened as he was, he could only smile as she tackled him to the bed.

"Careful, please, m'Lady!" Mel cried in exaggerated terror.

"It's fine," Aramis said. He returned Hannah's embrace and they stayed like that, holding each other for a long moment. Finally, Hannah released him and helped him sit back up.

"I'm so happy you are alive," she said. Her eyes welled with tears and one escaped, sliding down her cheek. Aramis reached up and wiped it away before kissing her.

"Me too," he said.

Lynessa cleared her throat. Everyone turned their attention to her. Her simmering anger was apparent. "Who is this *Hannah*?" she asked, glaring coldly at the her.

"She is my betrothed," Aramis answered, confused by Lynessa's reaction.

Lynessa stiffened. "Well ... congratulations. I'm glad that you are back with the living," she said. "I must be going. My army and my city are waiting on me."

"Thank you," Aramis said to her. "I know you had your own problems in Keswick to take care of, even after the Warlock had been dealt with. Thank you for coming to my aide. I am indebted to you."

Lynessa curtsied, her anger still noticeable. Then she turned and left the room.

"A woman scorned," Mel said softly as he watched her go. He looked at Aramis, wondering if there was more between them than Aramis had let on.

● ∞ ● ∞ ●

Lynessa fumed as she strode across the courtyard. How could he choose another woman over her? She had welcomed him into her bed.

Fine.

If he didn't want her, she would find someone else. She ordered her army to begin moving out.

As she led her army across the plains of Oakhaven, she watched the vultures pick at the bodies that had fallen in battle. She led their pace and they marched slowly home. Ahead, something caught her attention on the road. As they neared the form, Lynessa realized it was a man crawling on all fours. His head turned toward them as they approached and she caught sight of the arrow lodged in his eye.

"Help him," she said, thinking he might be a wounded civilian. His clothes were dirty and tattered. "Let the healers help him and bring him back to me."

The soldiers did as she ordered and she welcomed him warmly, inviting him to come and live in Keswick. The man gladly accepted the offer.

● ∞ ● ∞ ●

Adamar heard the approaching army before he saw it. He wanted to move before they saw him, but he was too weak. His injuries had taken their toll and it was all he could do to crawl as slowly as he was. When he heard the lady order her men to help him, he smiled. He knew someone would take him in. Someone *always* took him in.

● ∞ ● ∞ ●

Jovanna could feel herself drifting along the currents

of magic. Everything around her looked real, but it all felt different. Someone was there, just out of her sight. When she tried to see who it was, the shadow moved, always staying out of sight. After a while, she gave up.

Time was nonexistent.

Eventually, she began to feel weighted down again. Once, her eyes fluttered open and she glimpsed a stone chamber. She had grown accustomed to the darkness and wondered if death blinded everyone. Feeling finally came back to her, and she could feel her muscles. They ached and felt like fire when they twitched.

And then her eyes opened again, and this time they stayed open. Her gaze took in every detail of every stone above her. The small grooves and cracks, the cobwebs, everything.

She was different. And she was not alone.

"I wondered when you'd find your way back," a smooth voice said. It was a woman.

Jovanna turned her head. The woman was beautiful. Her skin was bronze and her eyes were a vibrant green. She had flowing long hair, so blonde it was almost silver. Her wrists and ankles were adorned with gold and silver bracelets. She wore a thin, sheer robe which did little to cover her nakedness.

"Who are you?" Jovanna croaked.

"My name is Vashah," the woman answered.

"Where—" Jovanna's voice cracked and her body shook with a coughing fit. Vashah brought a bowl filled with water and helped Jovanna drink some.

"You are in my home, atop Red Mountain," Vashah said. "You came very near to dying after killing that elf."

"Tairu," Jovanna said, the battle a blur and her memory fractured. "How did I get here?"

"King Garrick had his physicians rescue you off the battlefield before they marched to Oakhaven. There was nothing they could do for you. You were beyond the healing of any but the oldest of us."

"Us?" Jovanna asked, confused.

"Wizards," Vashah said. "You are a wizard. A true wizard. Not like those who play at it in Palindrom."

Jovanna remembered that place. Cignus had taken her in and taught her. He never understood her, though. Never understood that she was *different*.

"Why am I here?"

Vashah smiled. "I'm going to train you."

● ∞ ● ∞ ●

As the weeks passed, Aramis regained more of his strength and things slowly became more stable around the castle. Servants got back into their routines and the castle quickly became a swirl of politics and business as usual. Eventually, most of the people found it difficult to imagine life had been any different the past few months.

Most of the nobles loyal to Aramis's father had been killed, replaced with younger men whose character was akin to Adamar's. After the coronation—a small ceremony with only a few in attendance—Aramis's first act as king was to remove anyone Adamar had put in power. They were given the choice to leave the kingdom or be locked in the dungeon. Most of them had accepted the first option.

Aramis also issued a decree that all the towns and villages that had been burned and attacked by Adamar's men were to be immediately rebuilt, with everything to be funded by the royal treasury. As the word spread, the people who had fled their homes slowly returned. Crops were replanted, barns rebuilt, and livestock tracked down.

There was still so much to do, Aramis knew, but the first steps were the hardest. He and Hannah were married after the coronation, and since they didn't have the time to get away from their duties, Aramis promised Hannah a lavish honeymoon once things in the kingdom were back in order. How long it would take, he didn't know.

Mel, acting as the Chamberlain until Aramis could find someone to appoint, began a spiritual journey to find a new god to serve. Aramis thought he was a fool, but he kept that to himself.

Each day brought new troubles, but also things to be thankful for. The scars of Mordum's war would probably never be fully healed, but only time would tell.

Aramis looked forward to a bright and hopeful future.

THE END

ABOUT THE AUTHOR

Richard Fierce lives in Georgia with his wife and three step-daughters. He is the author of seven novels including Dragonsphere. Feel free to contact the author.

Email: Richard.Fierce@yahoo.com

www.ingramcontent.com/pod-product-compliance
Lightning Source LLC
Chambersburg PA
CBHW030632190726
48286CB00008B/2489